Clear Water Treasure

X Marks the Spot

DEAD END KID ADVENTURES
D.W. POWELL

DP KIDS PRESS

244 5th Ave, Suite G200
New York, NY 10001
(646) 233-4366
www.DocUmeantPublishing.com

Clear Water Treasure: X Marks the Spot

Dead End Kid Adventures, Book IV

Published by
DP Kids Press
244 5th Ave, Suite G-200
NY, NY 10001

646-233-4366

Graphics and Editing by Robin Powell

Cover by Ginger Marks

Formatted by DocUmeant Designs, www.DocUmeantDesigns.com

Library of Congress Cataloging-in-Publication Data
Names: Powell, D. W., author. | Powell, D. W. Mystery of hte box turtle shell.
Title: Clear water treasure : X marks the spot / D.W. Powell.
Description: NY, NY : DP Kids Press, [2023] | Series: Dead end kid adventures ; IV | Audience: Ages 7-12. | Audience: Grades 2-3. | Summary: When a treasure box with clues lands on fifteen-year-old D.W. Patton's head, he sets out with his pals to follow the clues and find the treasure.
Identifiers: LCCN 2023007703 (print) | LCCN 2023007704 (ebook) | ISBN 9781950075935 (paperback) | ISBN 9781950075935 (epub)
Subjects: CYAC: Buried treasure--Fiction. | Friendship--Fiction. | Mystery and detective stories. | LCGFT: Detective and mystery fiction. | Novels.
Classification: LCC PZ7.1.P687 Cl 2023 (print) | LCC PZ7.1.P687 (ebook) | DDC [Fic]--dc23
LC record available at https://lccn.loc.gov/2023007703
LC ebook record available at https://lccn.loc.gov/2023007704

THIS BOOK IS dedicated to all that have come before me as storytellers. Those who sat in rocking chairs on the front porch, those who were at the campfires, and those who brought the reality of leaving and weaving a lasting message. Thank You!

To my grandfather, Charles Wesley Bibler, and all the uncles who always encouraged my storytelling and writing. Storytelling, to them, was a way to take our adventures in life and hold them close for others to share. Thank You!

To Robin, my wife, who has always encouraged me and helped me through the process of writing and the telling of a story—Thank You!

To all who touched a young man's life and taught the feeling of "home" when in the woods, Thank You!

CONTENTS

FOREWORD

MY JOURNEY INTO manhood often took me into the neighboring swamp and the peat bog that was there. The water was always crystal-clear since it was fed from a spring. It and everything in it would change when the old man who owned it came with a huge dragline to dig the peat from the sides of the bog. When he was done muddying up the water, it became clear once more and the animals, songbirds, turtles, fish, and alligators would return.

This is where I first learned how to use my imagination, to leave the noise of the day behind, and search my inner-self. Trying to imagine what I wanted to become someday.

PREFACE

CLEAR WATER TREASURE is mostly from my imagination. The people involved are some I knew, and some I imagined.

With the help of the Gator Tribe, D.W. solves an old case to find the buried treasure.

Into the forest
a BOY,
Out of the forest
a MAN.

–D.W.P.

INTRODUCTION

TRIBES

Each tribe needs leaders. Plural! They need connectors to bring outsiders in and the insiders together for a common goal. They need to share Vision, Values, Morals, Resources, and Disciplines.

D.W.P.

Strategic delegation is what pushes leaders to the top!

D.W.P.

We are and should be helpers, mentors, and guides in this world to those around us. Sometimes we will be disappointed. Our time isn't their time, and we won't understand when the gift is given and not accepted.

D.W.P.

Week 1

> "To find the treasure a spring you must discover. Dig deep in your soul to find the cover. Bubbling clear it will appear to you. Seek the bottom and you shall uncover the next clue."

I GO BY "D.W." and I am almost sixteen years old. Today is the first day of my summer vacation from school. They call it summer vacation. Vacation! What a joke! I won't be going anywhere but to work! There will be no vacation for me this year.

Today is the day I start my first real paying job. I have worked delivering the local newspaper and mowing lawns in the past. This would be all new for me.

I was told to report to the jobsite at zero seven hundred, seven AM in normal people's time. The jobsite's address was 1911 Magnolia Ave.

The man I would be working for was a friend of my father's. His name is Mr. Collins. Dad knew him from his time in the Army. Mr. Collins only used military time when he spoke, I had been told.

The job would entail ripping apart an old house built in the late eighteen hundreds and then rebuilding it with modern wiring and appliances and still make it look old from the outside.

As I rode my bicycle up the driveway of 1911 Magnolia Ave., there stood Mr. Collins, the man I was to report to. He met me halfway up the driveway. Holding his hand up in the stop signal, he looked me over like I was a young skinny bull in the pasture.

I could literally read his mind. He was thinking, "Could this skinny kid, with glasses, on a bike, really do the work I need to get done?"

He said, "Good Morning D.W., park your bike somewhere one of the trucks won't run over it or haul it away as junk. Put on that new carpenter's belt and hard hat your dad gave you and grab a hammer and pry bar from the work box. Then follow me. There is work to do." It was right then I remembered dad telling me Mr. Collins wasn't one for small talk.

I quickly pushed my old bike into the back yard placing it by an old oak tree. Buckling on the new carpenter's belt, I found it was way too big and would need a new hole punched in it to make it fit and not fall down my waist.

I found the work box on the back porch of the old house. I searched the tool tray, grabbed a sixteen-ounce claw hammer, a twenty-four-inch prybar and ran after Mr. Collins through the back door of the old house.

Wow! This would be a job to remember. It was hot already, ninety-five degrees in the shade, with a feels like temperature of ninety-nine degrees.

I was told I would be working in the attic because I was skinnier than the grown men and could navigate the old rafters easier. I looked up and knew it would be even hotter up in the rafters of the old house.

My first assignment was to climb into the attic rafters and remove the electrical wires from the porcelain knobs. I was instructed to save both the wire and the knobs.

The porcelain knobs were affixed to the loblolly pine rafters with a single steel spike in their center.

This was going to be a tougher job than what I was told. The Loblolly pine would be hard as a rock after years of heat in the attic.

Since the electricity had been disconnected from the house, it would be safe, I was told. It would feel even hotter! There would be no fans in the attic rafters, only the holes in the roof for ventilation.

I found a ladder and was handed a cloth bag for the knobs from an old guy with a shaggy beard. He had yellow teeth from chewing tobacco and a smell that lingered as he walked away.

The instructions given to me were to collect as many knobs, spikes, and wire as I could find, and then bring everything down with me. Up the ladder I went and started to work. Sweat started to soak the bandanna tied around my head under my hardhat within minutes.

After an hour and a half, the sounds of people working below me stopped. My first thought was, did they all leave, or what? Crawling from rafter to rafter back to the entry hole was a much harder than it looked to be. Lugging my sack of knobs, spikes, and a coil of wire didn't make it any easier.

Once I got to the entry point, I couldn't believe my eyes! Someone had removed the ladder! I yelled and banged on the ceiling with my pry bar to get the attention of the crew. They had all stopped for a mid-morning snack and water break and had forgotten all about me hot and sweating in the attic.

Mr. Collins yelled whose making all that racket? He and the whole crew were laughing as he came to my rescue. He quickly put the ladder back at the entry hole, while I sat looking down at them.

In between the crews laughing he explained that when someone was working in the attic, they were supposed to tie a red bandana on the ladder to let everyone know not to move it. I climbed down with the rest of the crew full of smiles.

"Welcome to the crew," the old guy with the beard said. Somehow, I knew that this was to be the first of many things I would learn this summer.

I walked out to my bike and retrieved my snack of cookies and refilled my water bottle from the well in the backyard. The water was from a deep well, over one hundred fifty feet deep I was told. It was cold and had a sweet taste to it. The chocolate chip cookies I had packed were a little melted but hit the spot.

When Mr. Collins got up from his seat in his truck, it was the sign to everyone else, including me, to get back to work.

At noon, lunch was called. I climbed back down the ladder negotiating the bag of porcelain knobs, steel spikes, and another coil of wire with me. The lead carpenter said I looked like a drowned rat and smelled like one, too. He continued saying to make sure to drink lots of water with lunch. Guess I was sweatier and smellier than I felt.

Lunch was the fastest thirty minutes I had ever experienced. No rest time at all. It was back up into the attic until the end of the day was called by Mr. Collins at 5:00. Guess I missed the mid-afternoon break.

He said, "Good work guys see you in the morning at zero seven hundred."

I was so tired I could hardly peddle my bike back to my house. My legs and back hurt from being hunched over in the rafters all day. Home was only just down the street, but it felt like it was a hundred miles.

While putting my bike in the garage, I ran into dad and he asked, "How was your first day as a working man?"

I must have looked pitiful because he just said, "Get a shower and put on some clean clothes, you'll feel better. The days will get better as the weeks go by. Drink some water, too."

The cold shower felt good. It did help to lower my body temperature. The clean, dry clothes felt good also. Dinner was great! I probably ate way too much and when I was done eating all I wanted to do was crash in bed.

Zero six hundred came way to fast. I dressed in pain. Putting my boots on was a struggle. I didn't want anyone to see me or make the mistake of complaining. I ate my "Breakfast of Champions", and it was off to the job site.

Day two went a little better since I knew what needed to be done and how to do it. Mr. Collins said it would most likely take me the rest of the week to finish removing all the knobs, spikes, and wire. He continued telling me that when I got that completed for the whole house it would be time to remove the cypress ceiling lattice strips along with the nails that held them . . . and he wanted those saved too. *How did I not know that was coming?*

The rest of the week flew by with work, sleep, and more work. On Friday afternoon Mr. Collins handed out the paychecks to the crew. He paid me in cash because he said he didn't want to carry me on the books.

I took the envelope and stuck it in my back pocket and rode home. I didn't open it until after I was showered, in clean clothes, and had eaten dinner.

In my room I opened the envelope to find Mr. Collins had paid me the same as the other men on the crew. Inside the envelope were two crisp one hundred dollar bills. $200.00! I was rich!

I knew I needed every single penny to pay for the insurance on my future car so I wouldn't have to peddle to and from work ever again. A couple more weeks and I would use the cash for a used car, a year's worth of insurance money, and some spending money for the next school year. Suddenly, the manual work in the Florida summer heat didn't seem so bad after all.

Saturday morning. I was up early to do my regular family chores of pulling weeds, trimming, and cutting the grass at our house and my Uncle Warren's who lived next door.

Finishing both by noon, it was tomato soup with round crackers crushed up in it, a peanut butter sandwich, cold, sweet, iced tea and sit and watch Sky King and Penny on the old black and white TV set in the living room.

After Sky King, it was off to the shower to get ready to meet Robin at the theater in town.

The theater was in an old-World War II Quonset hut with worn out seats and a sticky floor. Robin's dad would drop her off at three thirty and I still had to ride my bike downtown and try not to get too sweaty on the way. The movie was "Hang Them High" with Clint Eastwood. I wanted to see Robin and I also wanted to see the movie.

I had just gotten to the theater and locked my bicycle to the oak tree out front when Robin's dad pulled up.

Robin jumped out and waved goodbye to her dad with him saying he would be back at six to pick her up.

Robin was carrying a brown grocery bag full of popcorn and two bottles of Nehi grape soda. We walked up to the ticket counter and I bought our tickets.

Walking into a dark, air-conditioned place was a treat. There was no air conditioning at home. The seats kind of reclined but we could have cared less. The movie started just as we walked into the theater and found two seats in the middle section.

We watched the movie, ate popcorn, and drank our sodas. The movie quickly captured our attention. It was about an innocent man surviving a lynching.

When it was over, we picked up our soda bottles so Robin could redeem them for a nickel a piece at the Winn-Dixie near her house.

The time had flown by and it was five forty-five so we sat on the green bench out front and waited for her dad to pick her up. My arm hurt from holding Robin's hand during the movie.

At six on the nose Robin's dad came around the corner and stopped right beside us there on the street. He asked if he could slip my bike in the trunk and give me a lift home.

After a long hard week working, I accepted the offer. He put the car in Park and helped me maneuver the bike into the trunk.

By the time we were done, Robin was sitting in the middle of the front seat with her hands neatly folded in her lap. Her dad got in the driver's side, and I slipped into the passenger seat, doing my best to squeeze next to the door keeping as much space between Robin and myself as I could.

Robin's' dad asked about the movie and we both started to tell the whole story, talking over one another so much I am sure it made no sense at all. We arrived at my house and Robin's dad helped me remove my bike as Robin stood and watched.

Robin's dad returned to the driver's seat and Robin told me she had had a wonderful time. She started to turn and then quickly turned back and kissed me on the cheek.

She jumped back into the passenger's seat and they were off before I could mutter a word.

She leaned out and said, "See you at Sunday School in the morning!"

Sunday morning, I had a hard time getting up and dressed for Sunday School and church. The blisters on my hands had opened and every muscle in my body ached.

My mom yelled it was time to load up and go.

So, I gingerly made my way down and out to the car.

I climbed into my assigned seat in the back of the station wagon and off we went.

Other than getting to spend time with Robin at Sunday School, the morning drug on.

Church was boring and the preacher from Texas was way off-base from the way I had read the Good Book.

After services, a quick walk around the church grounds with Robin and it was time to leave.

It would be another week of work before we talked or saw each other again.

With a quick squeeze of her hand and a goodbye it was back to the station wagon for the trip home. Home to a Sunday dinner of sauerkraut, pork chops, and mashed potatoes with Uncle Warren, and Uncle Lew, and the rest of my family.

WEEK 2

ARRIVING AT ZERO-SEVEN-HUNDRED at the old house, I found a cup of strong black coffee waiting for me. Mr. Collins had bought the whole crew coffee to start off the week. He took time to lay out the plans for the day and the rest of the week with each of us on the crew. He told us exactly what needed to be completed and who would be doing what.

I was to finish gathering the porcelain knobs, steel spikes, and wire and then get started on the cypress slats. I worked hard and finished up the porcelain knobs, spikes, and wire by lunch. After lunch it was back up the ladder into the attic and start on the cypress slats.

Using the prybar and a hammer, I was able to remove the cypress slats and nails saving them both with not too much muscle or sweat. Removing the old nails that held them in place was a much harder and blister popping opportunity than I expected.

The true two by eight rafters were loblolly pine and had dried hard as a rock. When one of the nail heads would break off, I would have to use the claw at the other end of the hammer. Sometimes I would have to resort to lineman's pliers and the crowbar to get them out.

It turned out to be a long hot afternoon making more blisters and pulling stubborn nails.

After work, I rode my bike downtown right to the bank in town. There I met with the bank manager, Mr. Fisher, and opened my very own bank account.

Mr. Fisher was impressed that I put the whole two hundred dollars in the account. He processed the transaction and handed me my brand-new bank passbook.

Tuesday started with me not wanting to go back up in the attic and work on saving more cypress slats and pulling nails out of those hard boards. So far, I had only finished one room. One of the old timers came to my rescue and showed me how to use the keyhole located in the back side of the pry bar to do everything like remove the nails easily.

He loaned me a prybar with a much longer handle and showed me how to get the best leverage on the old stubborn nail heads.

With the new knowledge, I was able to pull nails with very little effort and no more new blisters. I was able to finish every ceiling by Friday afternoon. The rest of the crew was impressed that I had stuck to one of the worst jobs that needed to be done.

It had been another long, sweaty, bone tiring week. Another payday made it all seem worthwhile and after a short detour to the bank, I was on the way home. I deposited all but twenty percent of my pay. I needed a little money for some new work jeans.

The ride home took longer than expected. The Friday afternoon traffic was horrendous. So many people down for their summer vacations on the beach I had to be careful not to get run over.

Saturday I was up with the sun to get the work done. That was one of my Uncle Warren's favorite sayings.

After I had mowed both yards, I would be spending time in Uncle Warren's wood shop.

I had been working on making a cutting board and needed to butt two boards together to make it big enough. Uncle Warren showed me how the jointer worked and then how to glue and use the pipe clamps to hold the whole thing together to dry.

Home for a shower and lunch, a quick nap and I was biking off to the mall just three miles away to meet Robin. Shopping for anything wasn't high on my list of fun things to do.

I met Robin and her dad at the food court at 4:00. When I told her dad that we were going to shop for work jeans he suggested that he take us down to the local Good Will store since the pants were to be used for work, why wear new ones?

Robin chimed in and reminded me that they would be much cheaper and just as good.

Off we went to the Good Will store. Robin found three pairs of jeans for what I would have paid for one new pair at the mall. The ride back to the mall was full of laughter and good conversation.

It was almost six when I was dropped off at the mall. With a smile and an "I'll see you tomorrow", I was soon on my bike peddling my way back home.

I arrived just as the family was sitting down for dinner. The conversation turned to my buying work clothes at the Good Will store and how much time I was spending with Robin and her dad. After dinner I spent some time reading a book on native Florida plants and animals.

Sunday, what I thought should be a day of rest and relaxation wasn't to be. Sunday School was a bust because Robin didn't feel good and stayed home. Church, well it lasted way too long.

Back home to change into work clothes, eat a bite of lunch and it was over to Uncle Warren's to work on the cutting board. We took off the clamps and I had to sand off the glue that had run out over the butted edges.

I had drawn out the design of a pig on a piece of white butcher paper. Taping the cut-out design on the board was the easy part. Cutting the large pig design out on the bandsaw was a whole other situation.

With a gentle hand, Uncle Warren showed me how to negotiate the curved and straight cuts.

We were running out of time, so we decided the pig cutting board would have to wait until I had more time. It was time to get the shop and us cleaned up and ready for Sunday dinner.

We walked in a little late to dinner, but I was with Uncle Warren, so no one said a word about it.

After dinner, a shower, and some more reading, it was time to get ready for another week at work.

I took the time to lay out my work clothes and boots so I wouldn't have to hunt for everything when I was barely awake.

WEEK 3

I WAS UP, dressed, had breakfast, and at the job site by zero seven hundred ready to work. Mr. Collins told me I had done decent work so far. He had checked the attic rafters and said there were a few boards I had missed that needed to be taken out.

"No problem", I replied and went to the supply trailer to picked up a ladder and the rest of the tools I would need.

Carrying the ladder and tools was a chore. I would need everything before getting back up in the attic. I set up the ladder and tied my red bandanna on the step at eye level. Tool belt on and supplied with a bag for nails, pry bar, and my trusty Estwing twenty-ounce hammer with the leather grip I had found at a yard sale, up I went, crawling over the rafters to where Mr. Collins had said the boards were located.

Once in position, I hammered in the pry bar and pulled with all my might. The board pulled loose in a cloud of old dust and yuck. The next thing I knew a small wooden box came down from behind the board and hit me square in the chest almost knocking me out of the rafters.

I screamed and the crew all came running and stood below me thinking I was going to fall through between the ceiling rafters.

I heard Mr. Collins call up, "Are you okay?"

"I think so."

Mr. Collins told me in no uncertain words to get the heck down so he could check to make sure I was okay.

Creeping back across the rafters was no problem. I was now used to negotiating my way around the attic.

Going down the ladder I realized that the box or board must have hit me harder than I knew because I saw blood on the front of my shirt. I handed down the board and then the box.

Once safely on the ground and sitting down, Mr. Collins said, "Pull up your shirt. Let's have a look."

It was just a small cut and had already stopped bleeding. One of the old workmen handed me the box.

Mr. Collins said, "Open it and see if it was worth the scare, you gave us."

The box was no ordinary box. It looked like the custom hand-made boxes granddad and Uncle Warren made for people's ashes after they were cremated. What made it different was, it had a latch that would need a key—a skeleton key.

One of the old guys said, "No worries. Use your awl and click the latch."

Sure enough, the tip of the awl fit into the slot and with a little persuasion popped the latch. We were all excited to see if there was money or jewels in the box. No such luck. Inside was an old, yellowed paper with some handwriting on it. Everyone laughed and Mr. Collins said, "Back to work. D.W., you can keep the box. You earned it."

I took the box with the paper inside out to my bike, placing it in the front handlebar basket. Then it was back up the ladder to finish the job I had started.

I had gotten all the old boards down by the end of the day with no more excitement.

On the ride home my chest started to hurt. When I got home, I placed the box in the garage so I could take it to Uncle Warren's and see what it might be worth.

Taking a shower revealed a small cut and a huge black and blue bruise over my ribs.

I didn't want my mom to know that I had gotten hurt, so I said nothing. I put some salve and a Band-Aid on the cut. The trouble was Mr. Collins was a friend of my dad's and he had already called my dad to see if I was okay. So, by dinner the whole family knew how I had scared the crew at the old house. My sisters and brother thought it was a funny story.

My mom said, "I told you; you would get hurt working on that old house."

The rest of the week I worked with the crew on the floor stringers. Replacing the ones that were rotten and reattaching the ones that were okay using metal tie-in clips. Most of them were in good shape except for the ones around the drains for the bathroom and kitchen.

Working under the house was just as dirty work as working in the attic—and almost as hot. Before I knew it, another week was done.

I peddled to the bank to deposit my cash, then began the slow ride home. I was tired and worn out. I needed to shower, eat dinner, and crash. I did take some time after dinner to call Robin on the phone in the kitchen though. We didn't talk long. No privacy and many big ears . . .

Saturday I was up and at it early in the morning. After a quick breakfast, it was right to work in the yard.

It always took longer than I had planned due to the many trees my dad had collected and planted in our front yard. When I mowed it was like going in circles around the trees and then connecting the circles.

While cleaning the mower and putting everything away, I began mapping out what I would do the rest of the day.

First, it was over to Uncle Warren's to mow, trim, and weed then time to spend in the shop. Then, I would work on the pig cutting board.

I took along the box that had hit me in the chest to Uncle Warren's. When he saw it, he turned it over in his hands looking at it like it brought back some memories of long past. After a close inspection he asked, "Do you have the key?"

"No", I answered.

He looked and saw we had jimmied the lock. Frowning he said, "The old skeleton keys were pretty much all the same. Let's see if one of these works."

He went to a drawer in the workbench and pulled out a box of various skeleton keys. They all looked old and tarnished to me.

In a jiffy he had found the right one and opened the box. He said, "You know with a little bit of sanding and hand rubbing this box could be a real looker."

He picked up the piece of paper from inside the box and read it.

"To find the treasure a spring you must discover. Dig deep in your soul to find the cover. Bubbling clear it will appear to you. Seek the bottom and you shall uncover the next clue."

"Sounds like a riddle. Looks like somebody wants you to find something. What do you think?" He asked.

I had no clue. We placed the piece of paper back in the box with the key and set it aside near the back of the workbench.

Uncle Warren picked up my big pig cutting board. He explained because it was so big there wasn't enough support to hold the two joined pieces together and we would have to add two stringers on the back.

Cutting the stringers and attaching them with brass wood screws didn't take long. When that was done, the sanding began. I worked right up to lunchtime and headed back to the house to eat, shower, and get ready to go to the beach.

The arrangements had been made the night before when I was on the phone with Robin. My older sister had walked into the kitchen while I was on the phone and asked if we wanted to go to the beach. She said we could tag along since she would be picking up her friend that lived near Robin's house.

After lunch, we drove over to Robin's house and picked her up. Her mom came out to meet my sister and make sure we would be well-chaperoned. She told us to be home early, before six-thirty—dinner time.

Sister answered all Mom's questions and we were off to pick up her friend.

The beach was crowded with people. Finding a parking spot was easy since we knew where the free spots were by the fire department.

Unloading the car and carrying everything down to the beach area went quickly and we soon found a place to spread our beach blankets. The water was warm and beach sand silky. We swam and walked on the beach, enjoying our time together.

Before we knew it, it was time to go. We were packed up and on the road at five thirty. We made it to Robin's in plenty of time.

Robin gave me a peck on the cheek and leapt out of the car and ran to her front door without much further ado.

The ride to my sister's' friend's house was full of them giving me the third degree about Robin. Most of their questions I had no clue how to answer.

Back home it was a shower, eat dinner, read, and crash.

Sunday I got up, dressed, ate a quick breakfast, and was off to Sunday school. The sunburn I had on the back of my neck stung with a buttoned collar and tie on.

We arrived at church to find Robin waiting for us. You could tell we had been to the beach. She had a pink face, and it looked like her blond hair was even blonder.

Sunday School and church went fast as we sat together. It was all over entirely too quickly for my liking and now it was time to go back home.

The rest of the day was spent at Uncle Warren's sanding the pig cutting board. Uncle Lew was there egging me on with stories of all the wood projects he and Uncle Warren had made over the years.

After a filling family dinner, I helped with the dishes, read, laid out my work clothes, and went to bed, another week over.

WEEK 4

AS I RODE my bike to the old house on Monday morning, I wondered what week four would have me doing. I had over-heard Mr. Collins say something about me helping the electrician run all the new electric wire in the house. I had no idea what that meant but I was pretty sure it meant working in the attic again.

When I arrived and stowed my bike, I was met by a tall, skinny man who introduced himself as Mr. Gurkey. He was the electrician and said I would be with him for the week. We shook hands and I followed him out to his truck. Inside the back of his truck were several boxes of different kinds of wire. He took time to explain the color of the boxes. He explained that the color of the box told him what size or gauge the wire was inside. That way I could get what was needed when he asked for it.

Then he pointed at a rack with rolls of single gauge wire on it and said, "Grab that and follow me."

Mr. Gurkey carried the big, gray, metal electrical connection box into the garage. We would first have to mount the box on the garage wall. It turned out mounting it was a lot harder than either of us expected.

With the box mounted, by lunch time, we sat at a makeshift table to eat our lunch. Mr. Gurkey unrolled a large set of prints tinged blue.

Blueprints he called them. He said I would need to learn how to read them even though he would be with me the whole week.

He explained the wiring diagram to me, how to read it, where we would have to pull wire and what gauge of wire we would be using. It also had markings where all of the wall outlets and switch plates belonged.

He showed me a funny looking tool to bend the metal conduit that the wire would run though. I would have to learn how to use the tool to bend the conduit so we could run the wire to the wall outlets.

The conduit bending tool was much more difficult to maneuver than when Mr. Gurkey had shown me on some scrap pieces of conduit.

After a few missed bends and some disappointed language, I was able to measure and make the correct bends in the conduit that Mr. Gurkey needed.

Every day it was up and down ladders, drilling holes, placing, and mounting outlets, bending conduit, and crawling through the attic. At the end of every-day Mr. Gurkey said I was doing a good job being his helper.

On Friday the power company came and ran the feeder line to the electric company's meter on the side of the garage and Mr. Gurkey finished wiring the electric panel. That was it, another week done.

Mr. Collins was happy with my work and said so when he handed me my pay envelope. The short bike ride to the bank was slow. I was tired, soaking wet with sweat, and pretty worn out from the work week. Every bone and muscle of my body hurt.

I finally made it home to a cold shower, clean clothes, dinner, and the best part, a phone call.

I called Robin after dinner to see how her week had gone. She told me of the babysitting she had done all week for a young boy with no manners, whinny, and a royal pain in the back side.

She asked if I was going to a birthday party for Jimmy, one of our friends from church.

I said, "I don't know anything about it. I guess I could go, he lives close to me and I could ride over.

Robin said, "Can I call you right back?"

"Sure", I said, "If it is okay with your mom." Her Mom didn't think girls should call boys.

She said, "Stay by the phone."

When the phone rang and I answered she told me, "Jimmy said yes, you are invited. Be at his house at three o'clock on Saturday afternoon."

After hanging up the phone with Robin, I realized I needed a card and gift before tomorrow afternoon. I ran into my sister's room and told her what had just transpired and fortunately she said that she had planned to go into town Saturday after lunch. Plans set; all I could think about was some much-needed sleep.

Saturday morning, I was up with the sun, dressed, ate a quick breakfast, and it was right to the yardwork: cutting grass, pulling weeds, trimming bushes, and watering the garden. So much to get done before it would be time to go into town with my sister to get a card and a present for Jimmy. What the heck would I get? Fortunately, I knew my sister would know what a good gift for a friend would be.

Saturday's chores were beginning to really be a burden on my time and energy especially after a long week working in the heat of summer, in an old house with no air conditioning, no fans, just a hot breeze now and then coming in through the windows.

Lunchtime found me again at Uncle Warren's working in the shop. I wanted to get the fine sanding done so I could get the first coat of cutting board oil on the 'pig', allowing it to soak in over the next week. It was time to finish up that project.

I had to hurry home to shower and get dressed to go into town. Having missed lunch, a sandwich on the run would have to do.

We were off to town. Sister suggested we go to Eckerd Drug store and get a card and maybe they would have an appropriate gift for Jimmy.

Picking out a card for a fellow guy was weird. Deciding to get him a fishing knife was easy. Eckerd's had both things I needed for the birthday party. A card and the present. Then it was out to my sister's car to wait while she bought the lady things she needed.

A short drive back to the house to do my best at wrapping the fishing knife, another thing I wasn't very good at. Noticing the time, I was off on my bike to Jimmy's for his party. I carefully laid the card and present in the front basket of my bike.

I arrived at fifteen after three, just in time for presents and cake. Robin met me at the door and Jimmy came running over to punch me in the arm and start the kidding about getting the invite from Robin. The party was fun, being with all our friends.

When it was time to leave, Robin's dad gave me and my bike a ride home. Seemed like that was getting to be a habit.

The ride home was full of good conversation and what we thought would be the lesson for tomorrow's Sunday School class.

Robin's dad helped me unload my bike. A peck on the cheek from Robin and they were backing out of the driveway and down the dirt road.

At home the dinner conversation concerned the weather and what was growing in the garden. Okra, pole beans, banana peppers and Roma tomatoes were all doing well. Mom added that there were a lot of weeds coming up and the garden needed tending. She gave me a look. Guess I needed to add the gardening chores to my list.

Sunday it was up and dressed. Peanut butter toast and chocolate milk for breakfast, then it was on to Sunday School and church.

I wanted to tell Robin about the box that I had found in the old house. I was working on and the cryptic message I found inside. The lesson of the day was about accountability.

In between Sunday School and church, we had a little time and I started telling the whole story of getting hit in the chest by the box and the message inside to Robin. She was obviously concerned about me getting hurt. Jimmy overhead us talking and wanted to hear the news also.

I took the message out of my Bible where I had placed the paper to keep it safe and showed it to Robin and Jimmy. She studied it and was silent for what seemed an hour only it was just a few minutes.

When she finally spoke, she said it was a riddle about where something was hidden, buried, or sunk under water.

She then read it aloud to see if it made better sense to Jimmy, her, or me hearing it read out loud.

"To find the treasure a spring you must discover. Dig deep in your soul to find the cover. Bubbling clear it will appear to you. Seek the bottom and you shall uncover the next clue."

As we were contemplating the words, we heard the chimes announcing the church service was about to begin. The three of us looked at each other and scrambled up the steps. We knew we had better get in through the doors and seated ASAP.

After church was over, the three of us decided to call each other during the week and brainstorm about what the message meant.

The ride home was a quiet one as the pastor's sermon seemed to hit home with those in the front seats.

After lunch I went to Uncle Warren's and put another coat of cutting board oil on the 'pig' and started stripping the old varnish off the box with ammonia and steel wool. I had to stop and open all the windows as the ammonia smell about knocked me off my stool.

I knew it wouldn't be an easy project because of the heat damage to the varnish the box had endured up in the rafters of the old house for so many years.

Family dinner was quiet, there were decisions being made about college and graduate school for my brother and the finances that went along with it.

I was tired. I knew I needed to get to bed early because I had another week of hot, hard work at the old house ahead of me. As I fell asleep, I wondered what job I would be assigned. Drifting off, I dreamed about what the message in the box meant.

WEEK 5

SUMMER VACATION WAS half over and all I had done was work. I did have a rising bank account with just about enough to pay for car insurance and the well-used car promised to me by old Mrs. Booth. It was also the week that almost pushed me over the edge.

I never minded working hard or even getting filthy dirty doing it, but while digging the sewer line I made up my mind that digging a trench deep to the water table wasn't what I wanted to do for a living when I got older. The bright spot of the week would be that my sixteenth birthday was on Wednesday.

Monday morning, it was already ninety degrees in the shade. Mr. Collins assigned me to be the plumber's helper. I thought no big deal. Inside work for the week. The plumber met me at the back of the old house where I had parked my bike and talked to Mr. Collins.

The plumber introduced himself as Charles Dinwhitty and said to call him Chuck. He was a large man with huge hands and a belly to match. He looked at me, hiking up his pants he motioned to me and instructed, "Follow me."

I dutifully followed. He handed me the end of a ball of twine and said, "Hold this right here on the outside wall of where the kitchen is located.

I did what I was told, and the plumber unwound the string all the way to the street, drove a stake in the ground and tied off the string. He walked back to me with a shovel in his hands.

He said, "I'll be inside working on the pipes. You need to dig a trench right by that string, sloping it right down to the street. At the street dig a six-foot hole big enough to work in.

"How wide do you need it," I asked.

His reply was, "Big enough for you to lay pipe in and make the connections."

"At the house dig the trench two feet down with a hole big enough to work in and taper the trench from two feet to six feet deep. Get started. I'll be back at breaktime to check your progress."

The bewilderment must have showed on my face because I had no clue why I would be doing what I'd been told to do. So, Chuck explained that the drain line had to have a slope to make sure the black water flowed correctly. He went on to say digging is what an apprentice plumber does while the journeyman does the inside work. He turned and walked away, and I started digging.

The trench took me all day to dig. I was dirty from head to toe. I had dug all day with only a couple of water breaks and a lunch that flew by much too quickly. I had the trench completed all while the older workmen walked by and smiled.

Mr. Dinwhitty came out from inside the material shed with an arm load of red topped stakes and a roll of yellow safety line. He dropped them at the trench beside where I was finishing off my digging and said to stake out the trench.

I was told to stake both sides and tie the safety line to them to make sure no one fell in the trench overnight.

I was sure that I didn't like this guy, but I had been hired to do a job.

On Tuesday I learned how to lay the cast iron sewer pipe and sweat the joints together with hot lead. Connecting the pipes was simple. Pounding in the calking took the time. Ladling out the hot lead took some practice.

The lead was heated to a boiling state using a propane stove with a cast iron caldron. It was so hot that when it dripped from the ladle on to my leather boot it burned all the way through to my sock! Luckily it didn't burn my foot since I got my foot out of the boot in time.

Connecting everything up together took the rest of the week.

The plumber said that starting the next week we would set the toilets, bathtub, and the shower pan. *Oh, what fun*, I thought. *A plumber I wouldn't be.*

Wednesday was my birthday. I was up before anyone else and rode to the work site. I arrived before anyone else and enjoyed some quiet time by myself.

My family didn't do much in the way of commemorating birthdays. I was sure there wouldn't be much of a celebration when I got home from work.

When Mr. Collins truck pulled in, he hollered for me to come to his truck. "Happy Birthday!" He said as he handed me a cup of coffee.

At lunch that day the whole crew ate together and each one had a timely gift. A pair of line pliers, a trench shovel, a pair of gloves, and cupcakes made by Mrs. Collins. It made me feel so special.

After a full day of sweat and laughter, it was straight home. I showered and got ready for dinner. My expectations were low when we sat down to eat.

After the meal there was some chocolate cake and presents. I received a new pair of blue jeans and boot socks from mom and dad. Sisters provided some English Leather cologne. Big brother gave me a new book, *Woodcraft*.

Thursday and Friday were a blur of activity at the job site. Trenches to be filled in and leveled with the final grading, more wire that needed run for the outside building and the outlets placed inside. I was learning a lot about electric and plumbing and neither appealed to me as a career.

Mr. Collins found me on Friday afternoon standing next to my bike. I was almost too tired to peddle home. I was too filthy to go to the bank and make my weekly deposit, so I had already decided to take my time and peddle home slowly.

I think Mr. Collins felt sorry for me and asked if he could give me a ride home. He had a project to talk to my dad about anyway.

I didn't ague at all. He loaded my bike in the back of his truck, I climbed into the pickup, and buckled up. I didn't remember the ride home. Mr. Collins said I fell asleep as soon as he started the engine.

It was good to be home and take a much-needed cold shower, scrub clean, eat dinner and just one thing to do after the dishes were done: call Robin to see if she had cracked the code and if we had any plans for Saturday.

Dinner was good. Burgers on the grill with Charles Chips and cold sweet tea. Dishes done, garbage taken out to the burn barrel, it was time to make that quick call.

Saturday. The sun came up entirely too quickly. My body hurt all over, but I had work to do. Dressed in shorts, T-shirt, and work boots, I had so much to do.

After a breakfast of Sugar Smacks, it was off to mow, edge, and weed both houses and of course tend the vegetable garden. I finally drug myself to Uncle Warren's workshop at about eleven o'clock.

Uncle Lew was there and greeted me with, "Boy, you look like you been beat with a hundred switches. Sit down and rest."

I said, "I need to work on the pig and put some time in on the treasure box."

Uncle Warren said, "Sit, you'll do no one any good if you are too tired and sore to work."

He brought over the pig to put another coat of oil on it. Rubbing the oil in was the least hard job I had had in what seemed like a long time. Soon it was home to some lunch and a shower. A short nap made me feel like a new person.

It had been decided on the call to Robin Friday night that I wouldn't see her before Sunday morning. She had information on the riddle, and we would talk about it then. The rest of the day I researched the words in the riddle.

"To find the treasure a spring you must discover. Dig deep in your soul to find the cover. Bubbling clear it will appear to you. Seek the bottom and you shall uncover the next clue."

The first word was "treasure". I found out it could mean a physical thing you could hold in your hand or something you enjoyed with your mind. "Spring" is a time of year or a source of water.

As far as "Dig deep in the soul", I had learned shovels to dig in the soil brought blisters.

"Bubbling clear", I am sure it means a spring, like out in the swamp. "Seek the bottom", sunk on the bottom of a spring?

Where do we start the search? The closest bubbling spring I knew about was Wall Springs up in Palm Harbor just north of where we lived.

I had been there before when I was younger. It was a cold, clear, bubbling, freshwater spring, and swimming hole.

Was the next clue to be found there? Was it buried at the bottom of Wall Springs? Was it the secret freshwater spring that is talked about just off the Beach of Honeymoon Island? I needed to talk to some of Uncle Lew's old buddies that had lived here their whole lives.

Sunday, I awoke with the book, "The Yearling" by Marjorie Kinnan Rawlings, lying under my back in bed. I had been reading it the night before. Guess I had fallen asleep with it.

I had to hurry and get dressed, eat breakfast, and be ready to go to Sunday School and church.

We arrived and unloaded the station wagon to find Robin waiting—not so patiently—on the walkway leading to the Sunday School classroom. As we walked to class—which we were late for—she talked a mile a minute telling me she thought that all the clues would send us to Wall Springs.

When she slowed down, I said that was all good. Did she know how we would get there? And did she have any snorkeling gear? You know at least a mask and fins. I had a mask and fins. I didn't have a weight belt or snorkel.

Before church we talked to my oldest sister Sue about the riddle. What we thought it meant and what we would like to do to explore the possibility at Wall Springs.

She said, "Church service is starting. We'll talk about it later."

After church was over Robin had to go home. I told her I would talk to my sister and call her later.

On the way home in the car with the family, I started to talk, and my sister, Sue, pinched my neck to be quiet. Later that afternoon Sue found me in the backyard working in the garden and explained that mom would never let us go there.

It was the place two girls were snatched and never seen again. After dinner my call to Robin went the same way. Her mom forbids going anywhere near Wall Springs, even if sister Sue went along and absolutely no diving.

I listened and my heart sank a little. After hanging up I made up my mind I would find a way to get to Wall Springs and dive to the bottom. I just knew I would find something there. At dinner Uncle Warren and Uncle Lew said they had a birthday surprise for me waiting at the wood shop.

WEEK 6

MY SUMMER JOB would be ending this Friday. There was still four weeks before I started back to school. The week dragged on since this week's assignment was working with the landscaper.

First, we had to dig up all the old shrubs from around the front and back yards. Then remove all the old dead grass from them both.

What a miserable, dusty, dirty job. My bandana that was used to wipe the sweat from my face was now used like the old west outlaws to cover my mouth and nose to keep the dirt out of my lungs. The shrubs had been there for years, with the roots so deep in the ground, they were hard to budge and even harder to rip out.

The landscaper had a John Deer 4020 tractor with a box blade on the back that made the job easier. Learning to drive the tractor and use the box blade to level the ground after we had pulled and dug everything out was a brand-new skill. Much easier than I had expected. However, it still took us the whole of two days to get the place ready to replant.

Then I began laying the pallets of Pensacola Bahia grass brought up from the sod farms down south around the "Big O", (Lake Okeechobee).

Next on the list was planting new red and yellow hibiscus bushes along the front of the house.

A small Live Oak tree was placed in the middle of the front yard far enough from the house to allow it to grow. It would provide shade in the years to come without the roots disturbing the foundation.

The back yard was just sod. The last thing we had to do was put up the cypress fence around the back yard.

Thirty-two post holes all dug by hand with post hole diggers . . . by me. New blisters, new calluses.

We finished late in the afternoon on Friday. It was almost dusk when we were done. Mr. Collins came to me and said that if I needed a job during the school year on weekends or even next summer to give him a call. There would always be a place on the crew for me. He handed me my pay envelop, we shook hands, and I rode my trusty two-wheeled bike home.

Arriving home, I had just enough time to wash up before sitting down to dinner. Everyone around the table wanted to know how it felt to work what they called a "real job".

My answer was, "I loved working outside and on a crew. I enjoyed doing electrical work, carpentry, and landscaping. I know for sure plumbing won't be a path I will be taking."

Later that evening I took time to open the pay envelope. What I found inside wasn't only my normal pay, but Mr. Collins had added a bonus for staying late and finishing the fence job. Nice Boss!

Saturday, I bounced out of bed ready to get my chores done. I needed to get to the bank before noon and ride on to the library. I wanted to do some research on Wall Springs and the girls that had gone missing from there.

The mowing, raking, and weeding went far faster than expected.

When I went back into the house, I was met by my brother who told me that I had gotten a call from Robin and should call her back.

While I had his attention, I asked if he was still friends with the guy in Tarpon Springs. I knew that his friend lived really close to Wall Springs and I was starting to make plans on how to get there.

I showered, ate some lunch, and called Robin. She wanted to know what my plans were for the afternoon.

I told her I needed to get to the bank, deposit some money, and then go to the library to research Wall Springs and the missing girls.

I heard her call out to her dad and ask if she could ride her bike to the library and meet me.

He answered that he had errands to do and would drop her off at the library. We hung up and I took off to the bank.

After making the deposit, I took a close look at my bank book. I had enough for car insurance and the car. Monday couldn't come soon enough. On to the library.

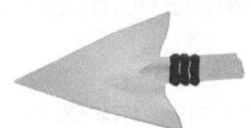

Robin was standing outside waiting for me. She said her dad would come in and get us when he was done running errands around town. We went in and started our quest.

Finding information on the missing girls was slim nor was it easy to find. The only information we could locate was that the two girls, both twenty years old, were last seen walking down the trail toward the north end of the park.

They were there with a scuba diving club that was diving in the spring. While their boyfriends were diving, they disappeared without a trace. Their blanket, purses and prescription glasses were still on the blanket.

The whole dive club was interviewed but no clues were shared by them. The search went on for days and the girls were never found.

We kept researching only to find out there was more information on pirates, fisherman, and bootleggers that had used the springs to supply their fresh water.

The Wall Springs Park had been made into a resort in its early years. A place to swim, relax, and get away. The old park had at some point closed, falling into a disastrous mess.

Then, after many years, the county cleaned it up and turned it into a family park for picnicking only. The spring had been walled off. No more swimming.

We found out by sifting through old newspaper articles that the park had dredged out the spring area and built a mound of limestone rocks that were piled at the back of the park.

We were at the front desk checking out books on the springs of Florida and the "First Peoples: The Mound Builders", when Robin's dad came through the front doors. He looked at the books and asked if we were doing a school project before school started.

Robin answered, "It is one of DW's favorite hobbies to look and find the mounds in our area."

Then he asked, "Would you like a ride home?"

"Yes Sir," was my quick answer.

When we arrived at my house, I unloaded my bike from the trunk and her dad said, "I guess I won't have to do this much longer, will I?"

I said, "On Monday I am going to take my driver's test, pick up my 1953 Chevy from Mrs. Booth, and pay the insurance. Not planning on much biking after that."

He said he would love to see the old beauty when I got it. He said he had one the same make, model, and year when Robin was a little girl. The ride home was full of information about how to take care of an old car.

I retrieved my books and stuff from the back seat. Standing outside the passenger side door, we said our goodbyes and waved at each other as I watched them drive down our dirt road. It always made me feel strange being left home alone.

I headed into shower, ate dinner with the family, and answered questions about what we did at the library. After dinner, it was my turn to clear the table, wash the dishes, and take out the garbage. Then, I headed into my room to read, falling asleep again with a book in my hands.

Sunday morning, I was up early! I was excited to get to see Robin and talk more about Monday's activities and my ideas on the Wall Springs adventure.

Robin met me in the parking lot of the church. She told me she had done some more research on Wall Springs.

It seems that it flowed underground from the main site out into the Gulf, about one hundred yards from shore. She was sure we would be able to find it easily at low tide.

This put another wrinkle in the information. Would the treasure be out in the Gulf, at the head spring site or maybe in the lime stone pile of what the Park Ranger called "rubble" from the dredging? *So many new questions and no clear answers.*

We got to class a little late and the other kids had some smart remarks about what we were doing to be late to Sunday School again. They had no clue that we had a lot to talk about and only held hands and had a couple of quick pecks on the cheeks.

After class we sat through the church service. When it was over, we had a short time to talk—with several interruptions. I never understood why people couldn't just leave us alone for even five minutes.

We said our goodbyes as I walked her over to her dad's car. Then, I walked quickly to my mom's car for the ride home.

WEEK 7

UP WITH THE sun to get the work done. Today was the day I was to get my official driver's license, buy a car, and pay out the money for my car insurance.

Sitting at the breakfast table, I looked around to realize no one else was there. They had all gone to work or a meeting in town or off to who knew where. There was no one to take me for my driving test at the Department of Motor Vehicles and no car for me to use.

I called my good friend Joey. He was a year older and with some fast-talking he agreed to take me and let me use his Triumph Spitfire with the manual 4-on-the-floor transmission for the driving test. His car was small, light, nimble and could easily do the three-point turn and parallel parking with no trouble.

Joey picked me up at 9:00 and we were off to the DMV. The line was short for the written exam and then the road test.

The gentleman that was grading my driving test wasn't happy about having to get his large body in such a little car. Much to my delight everything went smoothly, even the parallel parking.

We were out by eleven o'clock and it was over to Mrs. Booth's to pay for the 1953 Chevy Bel Air.

Mrs. Booth was ready for us with the paperwork to transfer the title and she even had filled the gas tank for me!

Joey followed me to Biff Burger for lunch, my treat. After lunch, he said he needed to head home and I proceeded to the State Farm Insurance office in town.

One hundred and ten dollars of hard-earned cash for a year's worth of insurance.

Finding a pay phone on the outside wall of the insurance building, I called Robin and asked her if I could take her out to dinner to celebrate.

While I was on the phone, she asked her dad if it would be okay if we went out to dinner together to celebrate the new car. Her dad wanted to see the old almost antique car I had bought and told Robin to tell me to come on over.

Arriving at Robin's, her dad was in the garage waiting for me. He walked out and said, "Pop the hood and let's take a look."

I popped the hood and saw her dad get excited. The engine was spotless. He showed me how to check the oil, brake fluid, the battery, and automatic transmission fluid.

We popped the huge trunk and he checked the spare tire. When he was satisfied that the car was in good working order and a safe ride, he called into the house to have Robin come out.

He then turned to me and spoke, "Have her home by ten o'clock."

"Okay. Yes sir," I replied.

Robin came out in jeans, a T-shirt, sandals in hand, and wet hair. Her mom was having a fit. Her dad said, "Get going. See you at ten. Now get!"

The time flew by. It was actually our first real date. We ate dinner at Red Lobster, rode along the beach, and headed back to Robin's house, all by ten o'clock.

I walked her to the front door. We had just gotten there when the front light snapped on and the door opened. A quick hug and she was in behind the screen door saying, "Call me," as the door closed.

The drive home was glorious. What a sense of freedom! I parked my new 'old' Chevy next to the rest of the Chevys in the driveway. My dad was a Chevy guy. Six Chevys all lined up in a row in our big parking area.

The rest of the week was filled with working at Uncle Warren's helping him build a new bedroom set for a client of his.

Every day was long, filled with new machines to learn.

Each one of them could be dangerous. Safety was the rule. Whirling blades could cut a finger off before you felt it Uncle Warren explained, as he showed me the missing tips of fingers on his right hand.

It was fun learning how to build using hand drawn plans on white butcher paper. The saying "measure twice cut once" is the rule for good reasons. When you make a cut on an expensive piece of lumber it had better be correct the first time.

The end of summer days passed quickly. On Friday afternoon once again, I started thinking about Wall Springs and what I would need to explore the head spring where it came up in the gulf, and that huge pile of limestone rocks too. I made a list of the three places I would need to spend time looking.

Saturday was like every other Saturday during my summer vacation. I did the yard chores like mowing, trimming, weeding, both our yard and Uncle Warren's in the morning. I made up my mind that today was going to be different. After lunch I was going to drive myself up to Wall Springs to explore the area.

I arrived at the springs about 2:00, parking the car under a shade tree at the back of the lot.

Walking past the huge pile of limestone rocks that had been dredged out of the spring under the new construction was interesting. It was much bigger than I had anticipated. Deciding I would go out in the Gulf first, I grabbed the backpack containing my snorkeling gear: mask, fins, and my new snorkel.

Walking the path through the trees, sea oats, and sandspurs, it was eerily quiet. The water was warm as I entered with my gear all on. The slight breeze made the water smooth as glass.

As I swam out the water temperature changed from warm to cool. The number of fish congregated there was overwhelming. I had never seen so many mullet in one place.

I spit into my mask to wash it out to make sure it didn't fog up when I dove down to explore the spring opening.

Taking a big breath, I submerged into the cold, clear spring. The depth was only about fifteen feet so, I only had to clear my ears once.

After many surface dives down to the bottom searching all around, all I found was a kind of slit that the cold fresh water came from and a bare sandy bottom all around the opening. I had found the exit for the spring! Nothing was there and if there had been anything to find, someone else must have found it already.

Wading out of the gulf, the air felt cool to my skin as I headed back up the path to the head spring a little way inland from the shoreline.

There was a Park Ranger there standing by a sign that stated, "No Swimming".

I thought to myself about how I was going to talk the ranger into letting me dive into the spring.

As I walked up, I heard him talking on his radio complaining that someone had dumped a bunch of junk into the head spring area.

I waited as patient as I could until he was done and said, "I overheard your conversation. I can go in and clean that up if you want!"

He answered, "You have any gear?"

"Yep, I've been snorkeling out in the gulf. I have my snorkel, mask, and fins right here."

The ranger made another call on his radio, talking on the radio for a few minutes, then turning to me and said, "The office says that would be mighty nice of you, go ahead. I will keep watch."

I grabbed my gear and into the water I went.

It took me better than two hours to pull out all the junk. I couldn't believe what I pulled out of the spring. There were bottles, cans, an old bicycle, old pots, pans, and trash!

After pulling in all the trash, I made as many dives as I could to make sure there was no hidden treasure there.

The Ranger thanked me, and I asked if I could come back and look for fossils in the big limestone rock pile I had seen when I drove in.

He said, "Sure, whenever you want. We really appreciate what you did here today. Thank you."

I had to rush a little to get back home and changed for dinner. After doing the dinner dishes, I took the garbage to the burn pile and then ventured over to Uncle Warren's to use the phone to call Robin.

Everyone was home at my house, so it was the only way to get some privacy. I used the phone in the shop to call Robin to make sure she would be at Sunday school the next day.

Robin answered the phone and started talking a mile a minute telling me about the horrible babysitting job she had. She had a ten-minute limit for phone calls, house rules.

When she slowed down, I told her about my week and the first of many adventures at Wall Springs that afternoon trying to solve the mystery of the note I had found in the box.

When our ten minutes were up her mom said, "Time to end the call." We said our goodbyes and hung up. Back over to my house to shower, read, and crash.

Sunday morning, I woke up and got ready to go to Sunday school and church. I was excited that I would be taking my own car and not have to ride with or be late going with my mom and sisters. I got there early, and now it was me waiting on Robin's family for a change.

I was there to open her car door and help her out. Her mom frowned and her dad said, "How chivalrous, D.W."

We walked away a few feet and she had a bazillion questions about the springs in the gulf and the head waters. I shared more about the serendipitous meeting and junk removal for the ranger.

The walk to the Sunday school classroom wasn't nearly far enough to tell her everything.

On the way into church, after Sunday School, I stopped and asked Robin's dad if it would be okay if I took Robin out for lunch and then drove her home.

I promised I would have her home by 4:30 since I would be expected to be at my family dinner at 5:30.

He said it was okay with him and he would smooth it over with her mom. We made it through the long sermon about helping one another. That put a thought in my mind I would share at lunch with Robin.

After church was over and some quick goodbyes, we were off to the closest McDugles for burgers, fries, and chocolate milkshakes. While we were eating, I shared the idea of adding some help to our adventure.

Robin wasn't too sure about opening the adventure to others. I promised she would like everyone invited and it would help us do the research, get prepared, and execute any plans.

A short ride down the beach and it was time to take Robin home.

When we pulled into the driveway, the front door opened and we saw Robin's mom standing there, arms crossed, foot tapping.

Robin wasted no time in saying a quick goodbye and she was out of the car and inside her front door before I could get out of my seat. The front door closed, and her dad came around the corner of the house.

His shirt was wet with sweat, from mowing the grass. He walked over and said, "Give her mom a couple of days to simmer down around here before you call Robin."

He went on to say he would handle it. I had no idea what he meant. I said goodbye and backed out of the driveway. I had no clue what had just happened.

I arrived back at my house at five o'clock. No one had even realized I hadn't been there for lunch.

Uncle Warren came wandering in at 5:30 and asked, "Who was the nice-looking young lady you took to lunch after church at McDugles?" He went on to explain, "I had lunch there, too, and you didn't even notice me. You walked right by me on your way to your booth."

The questions then came fast and furious from my next older sister. Everyone else just listened. I was glad when dinner was through, and I could take a shower, read, and go to bed.

WEEK 8

THIS WEEK I had promised Uncle Warren and Uncle Lew that I would be their best helper. We were going to build a new bedroom set for a client in Sarasota. I knew it would be a full week of long hours so we could be finished by Saturday when it was scheduled to be delivered.

Arriving at the shop early to find a steaming hot mug of coffee was a great way to start my Monday. I was charged with taking a long look at the plans for the bedroom set we were about to take on that were laid out on the drawing table. The complete bedroom set included two bedside tables, a standing chest of six drawers, a low set of drawers, a custom headboard, a matching foot board, and a cedar chest.

When the uncles wandered over to where I was at the drawing table looking at the plans and enjoying my coffee, I said, "Looking at the plans I am not sure we can get this all done by this Saturday."

They both looked at me and started laughing, saying they had only contracted to have the cedar chest done by Saturday, not the whole dang thing. The rest would take weeks to turn out. I realized that I would be there in the shop every day until school started.

After putting in a full day in the shop, cutting, milling, sanding, and cleaning, all I thought about was the treasure.

After dinner I called the tribe. *A "tribe" is a group of people ages six to sixty, male and female, who would help each other attain their individual dreams and goals while building long term, lasting relationships, and experiences.*

We call ourselves the Gator Tribe and meet once a week for fellowship and to plan activities. With all of us having so many things to do over the summer, we had taken a break from meeting. It was time to get together!

After several calls and call backs, we set a date for our next meeting to talk about the grand new treasure adventure.

Gator Tribe Fundamentals

Leadership Skills

1. Communication
2. Use your resources wisely
3. Know the characteristics and needs of the group and its members
4. Representing the Gator Tribe
5. Set the example
6. Plan
7. Personal performance and accountability
8. Evaluate
9. Effective instruction
10. Delegation
11. Personal growth

Our logo represents

Earth – Grounded

Wind – Change

Fire – Passion / Calling

Water - Transformation

The Gator Tribe had been together for a few years. Most of us were old enough to drive now and had cars, too. There are so many more things we can do together as we develop skills and memories.

The call to Robin was short and sweet because it was almost 9:00 and she wasn't allowed to be on the phone after nine. I asked if she was free on Wednesday evening for a meeting with the Gator Tribe.

Her first question was, "What is a Gator Tribe?"

I answered, "I will explain everything at dinner."

She quickly asked her mom if it would be okay, and the answer was it was okay as long as she was home by ten.

I told her I would pick her up at 6:30 and dinner was on me. We set the date for Wednesday and the place would be McDugles on the beach road at 7:00 since that was the tribe's regular time and place to meet.

Wednesday came and the day drug on. I was excited to introduce Robin to the tribe. I was pretty sure she already knew the girls, but not sure if she knew the guys.

I picked Robin up at 6:30. She came out the front door before I put the car in park. She was wearing blue jeans, a T-shirt. Her hair was still wet and was barefoot., Her sandals were in her hand. Her mom stood staring out the front window shaking her head. Robin got in the car, scooched over, and we were off to meet the tribe.

When we arrived, everyone else was already there. They had secured the back two booths that faced

each other. Robin immediately recognized the tribe
from school and church. I introduced everyone: Joey,
Martha, Tommy, Janie, Billy, and Jasmine.

When the introductions were over Jasmine looked
my way saying, "We have all ordered already, so go
order and we'll take care of Robin."

I asked Robin what she wanted and then went to
order our dinners. While I was busy ordering our
dinners, the other girls were filling Robin in on all my
faults.

The Meeting

We started the meeting with everyone munching their
hamburgers and fries. Sharing what each had been
up to since the end of school took longer than I had
expected. Everyone had worked a summer job and was
getting ready to start the new school year.

When everyone was somewhat out of breath,
I started the real reason I had called everyone together.
The treasure! I told the whole story about finding the
box and how Robin and I had worked on the riddle
and what we thought it meant.

Robin told the group about Wall Springs and my first attempt at finding anything in the Gulf and in the spring itself. I had printed out copies of the riddle for each of them. You could hear each person in the group reading the lines on their handouts and soon the noise from everyone talking over one another became overwhelming.

"To find the treasure a spring you must discover. Dig deep in your soul to find the cover. Bubbling clear it will appear to you. Seek the bottom and you shall uncover the next clue."

Our time was running out and the decision was made to keep in touch during the week with phone calls.

Our next meeting would be the following week on Wednesday to compare notes. Each of us would work on the riddle and promised to do some research.

When asked what my next move was, I told them that I had planned to make another trip to Wall Springs on Sunday afternoon to take some time picking through the pile of limestone chunks they had dug out of the spring.

All the girls agreed they would love to come and would check with their parents. The guys said they would do the same. Decision made.

The ride back to Robin's house was filled with ideas on how to mark the tribe. We had the logo already designed and she felt we needed to have some embroidered shirts and sun hats. It was nearing 9:30 when we pulled into her driveway. We were pleasantly surprised that the front porch light did not snap on.

A few moments of being alone brought on a hug and long kiss. SNAP! The light came on and Robin opened the door to the car and was out and inside the house with a quick wave.

I drove home excited that we now had a team who would be working on the mystery of the cryptic few sentences found in a box that fell out of an attic hitting me hard in the chest.

Friday, I worked all day in the shop with the uncles. I stayed and mowed the grass and went home to mow the lawn and do the other yardwork at my house. I planned to get my Saturday chores done a day early.

I barely had time to take a shower and eat some dinner before it was time to go to Robin's. We had made plans to eat popcorn and watch a movie at her house.

Little did I know that her little sister would join us. Robin's mom and dad had gone out to dinner with some friends, so I guessed it would work out okay.

The evening went well with cold Pepsi, popcorn, and a Western starring John Wayne.

I left at eleven o'clock and drove home knowing it would be a full day at the uncle's shop on Saturday.

Robin had gotten the okay to go with the group to Wall Springs Sunday afternoon after explaining to her mom that she would be with three other couples and never alone with me. I think her dad had something to do with her change of mind, too.

Sunday, I was up and dressed, breakfast washed down with a cup of coffee, and I was off to church. I was there early to greet Robin and her family and walk with her to our Sunday School class.

We both went through the motions and as soon as church was out, we were headed to her house. We had to take her little sister along with us since I would be at the house while she changed clothes.

Her mom and dad arrived about the time she was done changing out of her "church" clothes. They found me sitting in my car sweating in my church duds. Her dad thought it was funny that I had sat outside instead of in the air-conditioning. I just smiled as Robin emerged from the house so we could get underway.

Then it was to my house so I could change and pack a cooler with cold drinks and the makings of baloney sandwiches, chips, and some apples. We drove to Wall Springs and met the rest of the tribe. Everyone was excited.

The first thing I had to do was locate the ranger that had given permission to dig through the pile of limestone rocks. I told the group that if asked, we were looking for fossils in the limestone.

Martha spoke up and asked, "What the heck are we looking for?"

I said, "A box, enclosure, container, any hiding place something that might have been dug up unnoticed."

Finding the ranger turned out to be easy. He found us. After a short conversation he left us saying, "Have a good time."

Tommy told us he wanted to check out the fresh water spring spot out in the Gulf and needed a buddy to go with him. Janie was the only other smart one that had worn her bathing suit under her shorts and T-shirt. Off they went to the Gulf and left the rest of us to dig in the pile.

Finding fossils was easy and we kept some out in case anyone wondered what we were up to. At

4:30 Tommy and Janie found us all resting under an Australian pine tree drinking bottles of Pepsi.

They said it was fun snorkeling out in the Gulf spring, lots of fish, but no treasure to be found.

We decided we'd better get back home since it was Sunday, and everyone's family dinner was served at six o'clock. The entire Team was disappointed that we hadn't found a clue or anything else.

As we walked back to our cars, Joey kicked a lump of limestone about the size of a football, it went up into the air. It wasn't heavy like the other limestone rocks we had been sifting through. It came down and bounced once and split in half. There inside the fake rock was a key and a note.

The note was hard to read. It had become wet many times and was starting to fall apart.

Robin slowly unfolded the note and held it on her right hand. Squinting from the sun in her eyes, she read:

> "You have found the spot and that is a lot. The next clue for you will wear out your shoe. Safe Harbor is there – Indians beware. At the top of the mound, it shall be found."

Joey picked up both pieces of the rock enclosure and wrapped it in his shirt before anyone who might be in the area realized what we had found. We all walked quickly to our cars.

The jubilation the Tribe felt was hard to control. We knew that we would have to wait until next Wednesday to try and decipher the new clue. The hard part would be us all keeping the secret.

We said our goodbyes and went on our way to our respective homes. Martha had come with Joey in his Triumph Spitfire. Janie had come with Tommy in his old Ford Falcon pickup. Jasmine had come with Billy in his dads F-150 pickup. I was able to get Robin home and back to my house and ready for dinner by six o'clock.

Dinner was quiet. No one asked about the tribe or Wall Springs. After washing the dinner dishes, I was so worn out that all I wanted was a shower. It felt good to get the dirt of the day off. It also gave me time to do some thinking on what the new clue meant.

"You have found the spot and that is a lot. The next clue for you will wear out your shoe. Safe Harbor is there — Indians beware. At the top of the mound, it shall be found."

WEEK 9

ANOTHER WEEK IN the carpentry shop with the uncles. Every day was harder than the one before.

Calling the tribe during the evenings and checking in with everyone to make sure they would all be at our next gathering was more stressful than I had anticipated.

My uncles kept me so involved in the design and construction that I had no time to dwell on the new clue.

Wednesday came and with it a whole new challenge. The custom hickory slab Uncle Warren had ordered from North Carolina for the cedar chest wasn't going to arrive until sometime Friday, which meant I would need to work late on Friday to unload the slab and start working on it. It also meant there would be no Friday or Saturday night movie with my girlfriend in order to finish the Cedar chest on time.

That evening when I picked up Robin for our meeting with the tribe at McDugles, I wasn't happy about what I had to tell her about my work schedule.

When she got in the car she must have picked up on my glum mood. With a concerned look in her eyes, she turned to me and asked what was wrong.

I shared my tale of woe about having to work late Friday and Saturday. She sat quietly as I drove to McDugles. When we arrived, she looked at me and said, "Everything will work out."

I had given my word to finish the cedar chest job and I needed to be there. That settled, both of our smiles replaced our frowns.

The Meeting

Robin and I arrived a few minutes before the rest of the tribe drove in. Gathering at our regular back tables, the guys left the girls to place our orders.

When we returned with the burgers, fries, and sodas, we found the girls in a fast-paced decision making an agenda. Martha spoke up and said she thought the girls had solved the new riddle and had already redesigned the logo for our new Gator Tribe shirts and hats.

Billy started laughing and said, "We were only gone a few minutes and you ladies have everything solved. How great is that!? I guess now I can eat in peace."

Janie spoke up, "We thought the riddle meant to go to the Indian Mound at Philippe Park in Safety Harbor.

Safe Harbor = Safety Harbor. The sign says something like 'Indians Beware – Top of the mound = 'The Tocabaga Indian Mound at Philippe Park'.

Tommy jumped up saying, "I'll be right back." When he got back, he was holding a local map with a huge grin on his face. It was time to plan our next Sunday afternoon adventure.

We came to a united decision that we would all do our best to research the mound to get the facts about our next hunting place.

Tommy said he had Saturday off and could go to the Safety Harbor library to learn as much history as he could.

Janie said she would get a ride with Tommy and help him. *That was a good thing since we all knew Janie's handwriting was readable and Tommy's wasn't.*

We finished our burgers, fries, and enjoyed our cones of frozen custard. Waving goodbye to each other we all pulled out of McDugles and went on our separate ways.

I drove slowly taking Robin home. To lighten the mood, I told her I would do my best to call on Friday and Saturday nights after work if it wasn't too late. She said she would get the okay for Sunday afternoon and see me on Sunday morning.

After pulling into her driveway, she stayed in the car for a few minutes talking about us spending more time together. Before I could answer, the front porch light snapped on. A peck on the check and she was out of the car and through the front door leaving me sitting there wondering what had just happened.

Bewildered, I drove home. My oldest sister was in the laundry room folding clothes. I stood in the doorway for a few minutes, and she asked, "Is there something I can help you with?"

I blurted out about the one-sided conversation that Robin had started before the front light had snapped on. She laughed.

"What?" I replied.

"She wants to know if you two are dating or what?"

"What!" I was confused.

My sister went on to say, "Well you two have been spending Wednesdays, some Friday and Saturday nights, and Sunday School together, and now you're doing this new Sunday afternoon adventure together. She wants to know what you are planning. What does your future together look like?"

Now, I was even more confused. I wasn't planning anything beyond where the clues would lead us and school starting in a few weeks.

I took a shower, spent some time reading and went to bed. Wondering how I felt about a future with Robin, and what kind of future that would be, kept me awake for a while.

Thursday, we had an early day at the shop. Friday would be an even longer workday after the slab was delivered.

After work, I drove to the Largo library, where my mom worked, to do some research on the Tocabaga Mound in Philippe Park. There wasn't much information available. But I did find out that the park was named for Count Odet Philippe and his plantation that grew the grapefruit trees he had brought over from Portugal.

The mound is approximately one thousand years old. It was where the Tocabaga Indians gathered by the hundreds to feast on oysters and clams. The shells they tossed away helped build the sixteen-foot-high mound. It also said it had been disturbed and cataloged by archeologists from the University of Florida at some point.

On the drive home my mind kept asking one question: What would we discover at the mound on Sunday afternoon? I went to bed early knowing my Friday would be a full one.

The slab was delivered at one o'clock Friday afternoon. It would have to be cut into shape, sanded, and sealed before we could call it a day. Cutting it in half lengthwise took some time. With care and precision, we slowly and carefully completed our task. The two separate pieces would eventually become the head and foot boards of the new bed.

It took all three of us working to sand, glue, and seal them both. When I looked up from working, it was already eight o'clock.

I was covered in saw dust, my hands were stained with sealer, and my stomach was growling so loud Uncle Lew said it was time to stop for the night.

I dragged myself home to a scrubbing in the shower, a bologna sandwich, and a quick call to Robin at 8:45.

Robin answered and her first words were, "You sound really tired, are you eating?

I answered, "I didn't get home until after eight, showered, made a sandwich, and called you. It was a long day."

"Are you still working tomorrow?"

"Yep, and I need to get finished before dark so I can get my mowing jobs done."

With that she reminded me we needed to talk on or before Sunday. I agreed.

I was too tired to do it now and it was close to the cut off time of nine o'clock for phone calls. We said our goodbyes, I finished my sandwich, and went to bed.

Saturday I was up and off to the shop. I met my uncles as they were coming in and reminded them that I needed to be out early to do my lawn jobs.

They said that would be okay since only they could do the actual finish work that needed to be done.

At lunch I called my big sister and asked what I should do about Robin's questions. "Is there something I am supposed to give her or what?"

She answered, "Sounds like a good idea. How about that ID bracelet you have been hoarding?"

"Yea, I guess I could do that. Thanks!"

The afternoon went smoothly, and I was done by four o'clock.

The two lawn jobs were done quickly and I finished just before the sun went down. What a crazy week. I went home, showered, ate dinner, made another quick call to Robin.

She wasn't very talkative and didn't stay on the phone for long.

She left me with the words, "We need to talk in the morning before Sunday school," and hung up the phone. I had no clue what to do so it was off to bed with the lines from the last clue running through my head.

> "You have found the spot and that is a lot. The next clue for you will wear out your shoe. Safe Harbor is there – Indians beware. At the top of the mound, it shall be found."

83

Sunday was the day I had been dreading all week. The day started with me up early, dressed, and off to meet Robin at church.

For some reason I was running late and she was there waiting for me, standing in the parking lot of church, hands on her hips.

She said, "I had hoped you would be early so we could talk." She turned and started walking to class.

When class was over, I rushed outside and took her hand and said, "Let's take a walk."

She answered, "Mom will be looking for me in church."

I asked, "Am I still picking you up after lunch to go to Philippe Park with the Gator Tribe?"

She turned and said, "That depends."

"Depends on what?" I answered.

"On where we stand." She rolled her eyes and replied.

I dug in my pocket and took out the ID bracelet and said, "I was going to give this to you this afternoon in private."

She looked me in the eye, smiled, and said, "You can pick me up at one o'clock," as she reached out and took the bracelet. She turned and walked into the sanctuary, putting on the bracelet as she went.

I stood there by myself as she walked away. Deciding to skip church, I got into my car and drove home.

Changing out of my church duds and putting on blue jeans, cowboy boots, and a new short-sleeve shirt, I wondered how the afternoon would develop.

I had just finished packing the car with a cooler of cold drinks and ice when my mom drove into the driveway.

Next my sister sauntered by me whispering, "Mom is madder than a hornet. If you're going, you had better get gone."

I wasn't fast enough, and mom caught me climbing into my car. "So," she spurted out, "So, you gave little Miss Robin your ID bracelet? Do you have any clue what the means?"

I must have looked like I had turned into a crazy person, because I had no idea what she was talking about.

She went on to tell me, with her arms and hands waving in the air, "You have just made a promise to a girl!"

I was okay with that and told her so. I got into the car as dad walked out of the house to save me.

He said, "Go on. This will blow over."

I drove to Robin's house and was met by her dad in the driveway. He told me that my mom had made a fuss at church, and he was sorry for me and for Robin.

I walked up to the front door and met Robin's mom.

She didn't say a word when Robin came out holding her sandals in her hand, dressed in jeans and a red tank top. I walked her to the car, opened her door, and she slid in. The walk around to the driver's side was a quiet one. A wave from her dad and we were off.

The drive started out quiet and then Robin scooched over next to me and asked if my mom was still hopping mad that I had given her the ID bracelet.

I said, "She sure is and I am okay with whatever promise I made by giving you my bracelet." I wasn't really sure what that meant, but I was fine.

She said, "Pull over. Now!"

I found a spot on the side of the road and pulled over. "What did your mom say?" she asked.

My answer to her was, " My mom thinks by giving you the bracelet I made some kind of promise. I really am not sure what promise that is. From my mom's point of view, it means we would soon be engaged or something."

Robin started laughing. Between giggles she told me that a bracelet is like asking to go steady and we were already doing that.

She just wanted me to acknowledge it and make it okay to tell others.

She went on to say, "If you want to get engaged, you will first have to ask me, then talk to my dad and then give me a diamond ring. I think we are a bit young for that right now."

I looked at her and said all I could think of. "Okay. I think I get it now."

Back on the road we were both in a good mood and getting together with the rest of my Gator Tribe made for a fun afternoon.

Philippe Park was truly magnificent with its huge oak trees with Spanish moss dangling from their limbs, and cabbage palms. To top it all off, the view of the bay was one I will never forget.

Because of our brief stop on the side of the road, the rest of the tribe was already at the top of the Tocabaga Indian Mound searching for clues. Martha met us coming up the trail and said that the whole mound had been dug up by archeologists and she wasn't so sure we would find anything at all.

Tommy was sitting on a park bench drinking an ice-cold Mountain Dew and greeted us with, "It's about that time our leader and his mate showed up. We thought maybe you two had run off and gotten married or something."

The whole gang laughed. They had all stayed for church and heard my mom having a hissy fit over the ID bracelet. We formed a walking grid looking for clues while repeating the clue.

"You have found the spot and that is a lot. The next clue for you will wear out your shoe. Safe Harbor is there – Indians beware. At the top of the mound, it shall be found."

Once again, we thought we would be skunked, not finding anything. It was then Jasmine read one of the signs posted with information on the mound. She read aloud that there had been many artifacts taken from the mound and placed in the Safety Harbor Museum & Cultural Center.

Billy found a pay phone in the covered shelter that still had a phone book, a rarity indeed. He looked up the museum address and wrote it down. It wasn't far. "Let's mount up!" he ordered.

Off we went to see if the museum was open. No such luck. Their hours were Tuesday thru Friday 10 AM-5 PM and Saturday 10 AM-2 PM.

Billy and Jasmine spoke up almost at the same time, saying that they both had Tuesday off and could check out the museum and see if maybe, just maybe, there was a treasure inside their walls or at least another clue.

We all said our goodbyes after planning our next meeting at the McDugles on Wednesday at six. Robin and I took the long way back to her house.

She and the girls had gotten a big laugh out of the situation of the ID bracelet and what kind of "promise" it really meant.

I parked in Robin's driveway, and we talked for a few minutes before I walked her to the front door. We shared a quick kiss before the door opened. Robin slipped inside as I drove off.

Arriving home on time, Sunday dinner was unusually quiet.

That was until Uncle Lew, looked at me and smiled. Then said he guessed he would have to pay me more now that I had an "intended". There were some giggles and raised eyebrows.

Mom frowned and the rest of the family started laughing. It seemed that while I was gone for the afternoon, my oldest sister had explained to mom that a bracelet is just a 'going steady' thing, not a marriage proposal. Mom still wasn't happy, but it was a good thing to hear everyone laughing.

After the dinner dishes were done, I took a long shower to cool down and then read some more on the other Indian mounds in our area. Sleep overcame me and the next thing I knew it was time to get up and start the week.

WEEK 10

WAKING WITH THE knowledge that school would be starting next week, part of me was looking forward to it and part of me wasn't. Everyone around me wanted answers about what I would do with my life when I graduated High School in a couple of years. "What do you want to be when you grow up?" and "What college are you planning to attend?" were common questions being thrown at me.

I had no idea other than something in the forestry or outdoors realm. All I wanted to do at the moment was get a job, earn some money, and get out of my parent's house.

Monday and Tuesday were spent with the uncles working in the uncles' wood shop. They had decided that on Monday we would clean and organize the shop and get it ready to put the hand-rubbed finish on the furniture. It sounded easy when they were telling me about it.

Clean and put away all the hand tools. Next, unplug all the machines, strip them down to clean all the moving parts and get all the sawdust off each one first by vacuuming and then by hand.

Once that step was complete, it was time to sweep with the big broom, clean all the dust and sawdust up with a damp rag, and mop the whole place. All of that took the whole day.

Tuesday started out early and every piece of furniture was laid out on sawhorses to do only the fronts and sides by hand rubbing the finish on each piece.

By the time noon rolled around, we were finished with the fronts, and left them to dry.

Uncle Lew told me that I could leave, be he needed me to come back at 6:00 so we could finish the backs.

I asked if I could hang out with them instead of going home. I wanted to learn how to draw plans, figure board feet, and how to mix the hand rubbing material.

Uncle Warren spoke up and said, "Let's go and eat some lunch first and then we can figure out what we can do while watching the finish dry."

We decided on Big Bob's BBQ on the corner of Main Street and 1st Ave. next to the feed store. We drove there in grandma's old pink Cadillac convertible.

Smoked brisket sandwiches, crinkle fries, a side of baked beans, and a huge glass of sweet tea rounded out a satisfying and delicious lunch.

Lunch conversation revolved around discussing our next moves for the bedroom set. The uncles enjoyed poking fun at me about the bracelet incident and my mom's overreaction.

Uncle Warren spoke up and said we could use the drafting table in the house to start my next set of plans. It was decided that I could build several bird houses, using the wood scraps left over from the newly made furniture. But first I would have to learn to draw the plans, figure the board feet, and decide what tools and materials would be needed.

Back to the shop that was connected to Uncle Warren's house. The bedroom set was drying and felt like it would be ready early due to the low humidity and high temperature in the shop. The drawings were easy to make and I used the measurements from some old plans. Identifying the tools and a materials list went smoothly, too.

Figuring out the board feet needed was much harder. Length x width x height (or thickness) came to 144 board feet for the first batch.

Once that was done, we went out into the shop and started applying the next coat of finish on the bed-room set.

Finishing late in the afternoon, all three of us were dead on our feet from the heat and the work. We closed the shop and agreed to meet early the next morning for the next part of the process—the rubdown and polish.

After dinner I called Robin to make sure I would be picking her up for dinner the next night and the next meeting of the tribe. The Gator Tribe would once again meet on Wednesday at our usual spot.

The conversation was cut short when my sister announced she was waiting for a call. Robin and I said our goodbyes and I headed for the shower and my bed.

Wednesday was another full day in the shop. It was hard to imagine that the rubbed in finish and polishing took almost as long as putting the pieces together. My arms were so worn out I could barely lift them up by the end of the day.

I was able to leave a little early and get home to shower and drive over to pick up Robin.

She was waiting at the door when I walked up to ring the bell. She walked out in jeans, a blouse, with her sandals in her hand and wet hair combed back.

It was her kind of a rebellion against her mom's expectations for a "daughter going on a date". Off we went to McDugles to meet the tribe.

We were early this time, and it gave us a moment in the car to sit and tell each other about our week so far. Her babysitting job would stop once school started and she sighed when she said she was ready for it to end.

The rest of the tribe all showed up at once in the parking lot. Their laughter followed us all inside the building.

As the girls settled into our normal spot in the back two booths, the guys ordered the food and brought it back to the tables.

Jasmine and Billy were excited to tell us all about their trip to the Safety Harbor Museum on Tuesday afternoon. The lady in charge of the museum directed them to where the artifacts that had been removed from the burial mound were displayed.

When asked, she said she had heard a long-lost story of buried treasure in or on the mound, but had no knowledge of anyone ever finding it, though many had searched for it.

Billy asked if there were any more pieces in the collection that weren't out on display. The manager said she thought there were some in the back storage room somewhere and they would be allowed to search them out and have a look as long as they reported any significant finds.

Jasmine, knowing that the last clue was found in what we all thought was just a rock, kept quiet as they were shown the back room.

After two hours Billy picked up what looked like an old sword in a leather scabbard with a copper tip.

For some reason he withdrew the sword out of its home in the scabbard and out fell a crumbling piece of parchment.

Jasmine said it was like in all the books she had read. The strange ways people hid information and clues. She went on to say the paper might tell something as she grabbed Billy's arm and hushed him before he could say a word. Then she bent down and picked up the parchment and read:

"You have pulled the sword from its home. The clue did not fall far from home. Head south you will find another mound to explore and there you will find what you are looking for!"

After copying down the clue in a notebook, Jasmine carefully placed the piece of parchment back around the sword and slipped it back into its scabbard. They said it was all they could do not to jump up and down and do the happy dance. Instead, they walked slowly out waving goodbye to the manager who was with a tour group. She waved back to them and invited them to come back any time.

WOW! Another clue. None of us knew anything about another Indian mound south of us. How far south was the question on everyone's mind?

Janie spoke softly saying that she would be spending time at the Largo Library all week volunteering as a helper in the bindery and thought she could do the research on the area south of us and call us all on Friday to let us know if we had another adventure to fill our Sunday afternoon.

As we walked out to our cars, the whole Tribe was excited, yet disappointed and a bit let down because of the delay.

We had finished our meeting early and had about an hour to kill. Robin suggested we could park at the end the road and watch the sun go down over the Gulf and still make it back to her house on time.

I drove a little faster and we found a great spot to stare at the sun as it sunk down over the horizon.

Robin scooted over and announced we had better get a move on if I was to get her back home on time.

Driving her home, I almost always took the long way around. Tonight, it was the straightest route I knew. Home on time, no porch light, just a little sister pulling back the curtains and making faces through the window.

A quick kiss and hug and she got out of the car and disappeared into her house, leaving me once more wondering what had just happened.

I drove home slowly to another quick shower with the knowledge I would have another long day in the shop the next day.

I decided that I wanted to do my own research. I knew Uncle Lew lived toward the south. He had lived there forever. I wondered if he knew of any Indian burial mounds down where he lived. I determined to ask him in the morning.

Thursday morning found me dragging. I was tired and frustrated. I desperately wanted to do research, not rubdown and polish bedroom furniture again. I grabbed a cup of coffee from the pot on the kitchen counter. It was stone cold but would have to do.

I walked over to the shop to find my uncles drinking hot coffee and reading the newspaper.

They looked at me and remarked, "Look what the cat dragged in."

"You're late!" They said in unison.

I put down my cold cup of coffee, refilled it with hot coffee from the one burner hot plate and sat down.

"What the heck is wrong with you?" asked Uncle Lew.

I explained that I needed to know if there were any Indian mounds down where he lived.

His answer was, "Finish your coffee and when we get done with the work, I will tell you the tale of a treasure hunt I went on when I was just a little older than you."

With that said it was up and right to work.

Lunch was a quick affair, sandwiches, and a coke. The uncles wanted to deliver the furniture on Saturday morning.

We worked all afternoon and when we were done the bedroom set was gleaming and ready to be packaged up and loaded on the truck on Friday.

Since we had finished for the day and were sitting down enjoying our cold, sweet iced tea, I reminded Uncle Lew of his promise to tell me the tale of his treasure adventure.

He started out slow and easy. "When I wasn't much older than you, my buddies and I stumbled on an old treasure map at the local flea market. We paid a whole three dollars for it, which was big money back then. When we looked at it, we were sure it contained a clue about where the treasure was hidden.

"We took it home and used a magnifying glass of my mom's and went over the map, inch by inch. The hand drawn map did show a route, with a red X marking the spot of the treasure." He continued saying, "We tried everything we knew to match up the hand drawn map with a current local map.

"One part looked to be a way point, kinda sort a matching a place called Wall Springs, just south of Tarpon Springs. We rode our bicycles up to the springs to find it was a resort and you had to pay to get in.

"We waited and snuck in after closing time only to find no new clue and get run out by a security guy at the end of a shotgun firing salt pellets.

"We rode home in the dark and told our parents we were playing baseball and lost track of time.

"The next day one of the boys, I can't remember his name, said the route showed what he said was near the Safety Harbor Spa. We rode to the spa and looked around and didn't find a thing and rode home.

"There were some more spots on the map that were close to where my old home was and where I still live now.

"We checked around for a couple of weeks but didn't find any clues or treasure. We gave up and never got around to hunting the treasure after that."

"What happened next."

"Me and my buddies all got drafted into the Army and when we got home from the war we started careers, got married, raised families, and that was about it. Finding a treasure was a long-forgotten endeavor."

I asked if he still had the map. His answer was, "I think it might be still stored in the shed at my house. One of my buddies had placed it in a hollowed-out piece of bamboo and sealed the ends with clay. You can look for it if you want to after we deliver the bedroom set Saturday. We'll be driving right by my house on the way back."

Friday was another full day spent finishing the polishing and wrapping each piece of furniture in shipping blankets. Once they were nestled securely in the back of the big, enclosed truck they would be ready to deliver on Saturday.

We finished early so, I called Robin to see if we could maybe go out to the Drive-In to watch a movie. I heard her ask her mom and get a "yes".

She came back on the phone and said to pick her up at 7:30. She would find a movie and make sure we got there in time to see the beginning.

She went on to say she had to be in by 11:30 and hoped the movie would be over and I could get her home on time. It was a good thing because my curfew was midnight.

I went home to shower and change into some decent jeans, a T-shirt, and boots. Picking Robin up went smoothly since Robin's mom, dad and sister had gone out to dinner and to do some shopping.

We drove to the Mustang Drive In and got there just in time to get some popcorn and sodas at the concession stand and make it back to the car to watch the previews.

The movie was True Grit staring John Wayne, Glen Campbell, Kim Darby, Dennis Hopper, and Robert Duvall. We watched the movie, talked about what I had found out from Uncle Lew and the opportunity to try and find the map after the delivery the next day.

The movies ran over three hours causing us to have to rush a bit to get her home on time.

We sat for what seemed mere moments when the dashboard clock flipped to11:30 and the front porchlight mysteriously snapped on. A last kiss, a walk to the front door, a goodnight and I was back in the car headed home before midnight.

Home, a quick snack of chips, and off to bed.

Saturday I was up with the sun, got dressed, and hustled over to the shop. I had to wait for the uncles to appear. They had been to a late-night card game and were a little worse for wear.

They both spoke at once asking if I thought I could drive the truck. No problem, I replied. A sixteen-year-old with less than a month driving experience was going to drive a good-sized truck!

I didn't realize I would have to drive over one of the tallest bridges in our area to get to where we had to make the delivery. Uncle Lew made a fresh pot of very strong coffee and poured the whole thing into two thermoses.

We loaded up with me driving, Uncle Lew sitting in the middle as navigator, and Uncle Warren leaning against the side door with the windows down. No air-conditioning in that old truck.

When we got to the Skyway Bridge, I asked, "Are you two sure you trust me to drive over this bridge?" *I wasn't sure I trusted me.*

The response was, "Get in the left lane, drive the fifty-five miles an hour speed limit and coast down the other side. You'll be okay. It's your first drive over the bay but you'll be fine."

I was scared out of my wits, but kept quiet and drove. In no time, we were up and over. "Easy peasy!" I bragged.

Finding the house was no problem with Uncle Lew's explicit directions. Unloading and placing the new bedroom set in the house was a test of getting the pieces through the doors and narrow hallways of the house.

It was after one o'clock when we finished, were paid, and were headed home. On our way we made a stop at a McDugles and devoured our burgers, fries, and chocolate milk shakes for lunch.

We arrived back at Uncle Lew's at 2:30 and the hunt was on. I have never seen such a jumble of old stuff in any one place. This would take a whole lot longer than I had expected. With no luck after searching for a couple of hours and a promise to come back and help clean out the shed, I drove Uncle Warren back to his house and parked the truck.

I hadn't heard from Janie, so I called her as soon as I got home. She had just walked in from the library and her mom put her on the phone.

Janie said, "I was just about to call you. There is another Calusa mound in St. Petersburg!" She gave me the address. *It was the one closest to my Uncle Lew's.* She asked about going there Sunday afternoon, and I agreed, "Let's meet at my Uncle Lew's."

I gave her the address and she said she would call everyone else. I spent the rest of the day, until dark, mowing grass, pulling weeds, and trimming bushes.

At dark, I headed inside to shower, eat a late dinner, and crash. It had been a super long week and there would be more physical work to do after church.

Sunday and I am tired! Dressed in my Sunday duds, I head to church. My shoes could have used some polish, but they would have to wait for another time. When I pulled in, Robin was already in the parking lot waiting for me.

She greeted me with, "You look worn out. Do we need to take the afternoon off from looking for the treasure?"

I told her, "I didn't find the bamboo holder with the map yesterday and was counting on the whole Tribe to help clean out Uncle Lew's shed to help find it."

Sunday school and church did little to hold my interest.

Robin had to, more than once, jab me with her elbow to wake me up to stand and sing the hymns during worship.

After church was over, I drove her and her sister to their house so Robin could change. We left her sister watching TV, then drove over to my house so I could change.

We stopped at a Biff Burger on the way to Uncle Lew's for some lunch. Burgers, tater-tots, and Pepsi colas.

When we arrived at Uncle Lew's, he had already started cleaning out the shed. What a mess!

The rest of the tribe showed up and it wasn't long before we had the whole place cleared out all the way to the floor. Boxes and junk sat haphazardly scattered all over the backyard.

We swept out the shed and started to look through the boxes and load things back in as Uncle Lew supervised and had us stack what he deemed 'junk' outside in a pile.

We were almost done when Aunt Bea came out and said she and the girls had been inside cleaning out old junk and had found the bamboo tube in a carton marked "Keepers". Aunt Bea brought out some ice-cold, iced tea for everyone as we gathered around the table on the back porch to see what was in the bamboo tube.

The ends were plugged with clay that had disintegrated into dust over the years and it looked like the silver fish had liked the glue on the paper. Sliding the map out gently, Martha unrolled it ever so slowly. To say our anticipation was high, was an understatement. The map was in bad shape. There was a spot on the map that looked like it was close, real close to where we were. The downside was it was time to pack up and get home for Sunday dinners. The search would have to wait another few days.

Martha gently rolled the map back up and placed it into its container. She said she would do her best to restore it and make it more readable and let everyone know as soon as she had it done.

All of the tribe knew it was the last Sunday before school was to start. We were sure we could find the treasure during the next weekend and be heroes at the start of a new school year.

We all packed up and drove off. Robin's house was on the way to my house. After a quick peck on the cheek and a promise to call later, I had to drive quickly home to be there before dinner started. I made it just in time to wash my hands and slide into my chair.

WEEK 11

IT WAS THE first week of a new school year and I wasn't ready or excited to be there. Monday was a get ready day. I had put it off as long as I could.

There was so much to do. I needed some new school clothes. Blue jeans, some shirts, maybe a new pair of boots. Shopping was one of my least favorite things to do. First, I needed to take a hard look at the money I had left from my summer job and put together a budget with a list of needs and a list of wants.

Then it was off to the shopping center. After getting one shirt and a pair of jeans it was back to the house. Walking in with my bag of clothes and another with supplies, I was bombarded with questions. Everyone was home and ready to interrogate me about my decisions on what I would wear to school.

I eased my way out as quickly as I dared and walked over to Uncle Warren's. I found him in the shop. He was sitting at his desk holding the newspaper away from him so he could read it without putting on his glasses.

He had a cup of coffee that I am sure had turned cold sitting on his desk. I spotted Uncle Lew snoozing in his old reclining chair.

He looked up and spouted, "Where are you going and why?"

My reply was, "I need some time away from the house. I'm tired of answering all their questions. I need some peace and quiet to figure out what I need to do next. I have to decide what I want to be when I finish school and what I want to do now. The shop is as good as place as any."

"As good a place as any? Why, this here is the best of places!"

We talked as I wrote out my lists and discovered that I needed to find a regular part-time job. My summer job money was dwindling fast.

Uncle Lew said. "I would hire you, to do little jobs, but it wouldn't be regular." He went on to say, "I was down to Ed's American Gas Station and Garage to get an oil change this morning. Ed, the owner, told me he was looking for someone to work afternoons and to close the garage at 8 o'clock on weeknights. It would include an eight-hour day on Saturdays. Do you think you could do that?" Uncle Lew asked me.

Taking a moment to think, I asked "What kind of stuff would I be doing?"

Uncle Lew said, "Pump gas, check tires, wash windows, maybe change oil, change tires, and whatever."

It was only Monday afternoon so I drove down to Ed's American Gas Station and Garage. Ed was a short, thin man. His face was deeply lined from the sun. He had full, long eyebrows, hands stained black from grease, and was slightly bent over from working under the hoods of cars his entire life. He looked like a no-nonsense kind of man.

When he saw me parking and walking in, his first words were, "You're Big Bob's boy aren't you?"

I stammered and said, "Yes, yes, I am."

He wasted no time saying that my dad was a good mechanic and asked if I was as good with my hands and head as he was.

I didn't know how to answer. I had never met this man, having only had heard about him from my uncles.

Ed sputtered out that he was offering me an opportunity of a lifetime to make some money and learn several new skills along the way. He went on to say that if I worked out, he normally was closed on Sundays, but he would allow me to open the garage on Sundays and whatever money I brought in, I would make wages plus commission.

I will see how things play out before I make any hard decisions for my life, but as far as a part-time job, for now, this sounded fine.

"Do you want the job?"

Answering with reservation in my voice, "Yes, I want the job."

He continued talking, asking my shirt and pants size, and told me to be there by 4:00 or right after school let out. He could use the evenings to teach me what I would need to know. I was bewildered and shocked. I was hired without even asking for a job.

I bet the uncles had already paved the way. It doesn't hurt, I suppose, that my dad worked at the only other garage in town. I was to start the next day.

I drove back home thinking my life had just closed in on me. There would be school Monday to Friday. Work after school four hours Monday through Friday, with eight hours on Saturday at Ed's American Gas Station and Garage.

I would only have time to myself on Saturday night and maybe all-day Sunday. Life was changing fast.

At dinner that evening I told the family that I had secured a steady after-school job at Ed's American Gas Station and Garage. My mom said nothing, just gave me "the look".

I had heard her many times say she didn't want any more "grease monkeys" in the house. So, I knew exactly what she was thinking.

Dad wasn't at all surprised. Uncle Lew had mentioned to Ed that I might want the job. Ed had called dad to make sure it would be okay. That was that.

My sisters and brother all had jobs and wanted to know if they would be able to buy gas cheaper from me. I didn't let anyone see what I was feeling. I needed to talk to Robin.

After dinner, I cleared the plates and took out the garbage on my way over to Uncle Warren's shop. I didn't want the family to know that I was feeling trapped into a life that I wasn't sure I wanted.

On the short walk I tried to pull my thoughts together. What was it that was nagging at me? I knew Robin would help me see the bright side of it all.

I entered the shop from the side door and sat in the dark at the big old oak desk where the phone rested. Picking it up, I dialed Robin's number. Her little sister answered the phone. So, I asked if I could speak to Robin.

I heard a clunk of the phone receiver hitting the floor and the yell from the bottom of her sister's lungs that the phone was for Robin. The phone went quiet and then a shuffle of feet, and moments later Robin picked up the phone.

She apologized for her sister and told me she had been back in her room finishing sewing some clothes for the start of the new school year.

I listened to her tell me about the shopping trip to the fabric store and all the material she had gotten, along with new patterns, zippers, thread, and other stuff.

I had no clue what they were or what they were for.

When she ran out of steam, I told her, "I have taken a job to work at Ed's American Gas Station and Garage. I will be working every afternoon after school from four to eight and eight hours on Saturdays."

Robin was quiet and then said, "That means we can only see each other on the way to and from school, Saturday nights, and maybe Sundays."

"Yep!"

She knew that I supported myself and paid for my car, insurance, gas, spending money, clothes, and saving for the future, along with dates with her.

"Well, we'll just have to make it work. Will you be picking me up for the first day of school tomorrow or should I plan on riding the bus?"

"You need to ask your mom about the ride to school and ask if your curfew for Friday nights can be extended to 11:30. While you are at it, make sure it's okay for you to ride to school and home with me. Okay?"

It was then I heard her dad come in and say it was time to say goodnight and get off the phone.

Monday had been a long exhausting day. I was concerned about Tuesday morning going to school and in the afternoon learning all the new things and how to close the garage at the end of the day.

Tuesday. Up and dressed, a quick breakfast, and I was off to pick up Robin. Seeing her in the morning was a good way to start the day.

The first day of the new school year went as expected. The anxiety of getting used to the new schedule, meeting the new teachers, and deciding whether to stay in school or drop out.

After the ending bell, I met Robin at the car and drove her home. I had to hustle to get home myself, eat a snack, and get to the garage by 4:00.

Arriving right on time, I was welcomed with a cup of the strongest coffee I had ever ingested. It was so thick I asked how long it had been on the burner.

Mr. Ed answered, "Frankly, I think it might be left over from yesterday." *It could even have been from the day before.*

I drank the terrible coffee while learning how to use the cash register. It had certain buttons for things we sold like for gas, tires, batteries & accessories. There was even one for miscellaneous.

There were special books for certain customers that ran a tab. They paid once a month. Their purchases were to be rung up and their names written on the tally sheet for the day.

Before I knew it, it was dinner time. Buddy, the mechanic, went across the street to Charlie & Millie's Pizza and got a large pizza with the works on it.

Two pieces of pizza and an orange soda from the old Coke machine that sat out in front of the station made a mighty fine dinner.

We were no sooner done when a step truck pulled in marked 'Uniform Service' and a really tall fellow bounced out of the truck and measured me for pants and shirts.

Mr. Ed said they would be ready by the time I got there the next Monday, my official start day. He asked if I could come back in Wednesday after school since he and Buddy had scheduled two oil changes and a tire rotation and thought it would be a valuable thing for me to learn.

"Yes Sir! I'll see you tomorrow." Nodding, Mr. Ed ushered me out the door saying they had work to get done.

I drove home to shower and change. I wanted to call Robin, but I knew she was babysitting again until nine o'clock. So, instead I decided to go to the library since I had a little time. I wanted to see what other information I might find on the Tocabaga natives and their mounds in the area.

I arrived just in time to get two books checked out and leave before they closed for the night.

At home, I poured over local old maps and searched through the books I had gathered. What I discovered was that there were as many mounds in and around our town as there were fingers on both of my hands.

I sat on my bed with a new local map, more questions than answers and wondering what the rest of the tribe had discovered.

Wednesday started out with driving Robin to school. It was a quiet ride. Both of us were caught in our own thoughts of how the day would go.

As we pulled into the school parking lot, I saw Joey standing next to his car. I asked if he or Martha had found any new information on which mound, we needed to search. He told me they hadn't worked on it but would have something to report on that evening at our gathering spot.

Seeing Tommy, we walked over to find out what he and Janie had come up with, if anything. They had no more information either. They confirmed that they would be at the meeting that evening though.

Meeting Billy in the hallway outside his class, he said that he and Jasmine had visited Weedon Island Preserve and Natural History Center. They spent time walking the area and studying the map they found in a box at the head of the trail.

After several mosquito bites and one mishap of walking into a huge Golden Silk or "banana" spider's web, they had left with the feeling that the next place to go was Indian Mound Park at Maximo Point.

The day seemed to drag on forever. Robin met me in the school parking lot after the last bell and I drove her home sharing the news from the tribe.

As I drove she told me of all the terrible things the little brat of a boy had done the night before to torment her while she was babysitting.

She went on till there was a break in her monologue and I asked, "Are we still on for our Wednesday dinner and meeting with the tribe?"

"I've already cleared it with my mom so you can pick me up at six o'clock."

"I will do my best! I will be at the garage in the afternoon learning how to change out and mount tires."

She looked at me and said, "Take a shower and wash the grease from your hands first, please." I looked over at her and we both burst out laughing.

I filled her in about what Billy and Jasmine had found out and what they said about there being several mounds in our area.

Robin said she was afraid that there were too many to search, and asked if we did find something, did we have to turn it over to the state.

I had no answers. More to research.

Robin added that she thought she might be able to get some answers from the father of the 'little monster' she was babysitting since he was a lawyer.

After school on Wednesday I headed to Ed's after dropping Robin off at her house.

The afternoon flew by. I never knew that I would be so overloaded with learning how to change the oil and oil filter on a car.

First, I had to learn how to drive the car in on the rack. Lining the car up on the rack had to be perfect before setting the risers and raising the car off the ground.

At 5:45 I hopped in my car and drove as fast as I could to make a short visit to Uncle Lew's. After a quick conversation about work, I had to hustle to get ready to pick up Robin for our meeting and dinner.

I arrived at Robin's right at 6:15. I was fifteen minutes late! It wasn't something I was in the habit of doing. She was waiting at the door when I walked up and knocked.

I don't know what was happening inside, but she grabbed my hand and hurried me to the car.

Once we were down the road, she told me that the heated discussion was about why she always left the house with wet hair and bare feet.

I thought it was kind of funny. Her look told me it was not the least bit funny.

The real reason was just her way of voicing her protest to her mom because she still thought Robin should wear a dress, panty hose, and style her hair when we went out. Times had changed and she would have looked weird dressed that way.

We met the rest of the tribe at our usual hang out at 6:30. The guys ordered the

dinners and the girls got settled in our coveted spot in the back of the dining area.

As I gathered our food and walked back to the table, I heard Jasmine talking about her and Billy's adventure at Weedon Island and the encounter with the biggest spider she had ever seen. She held her hands together making a circle saying that the spider was even bigger than her hands put together.

She went on to say that Billy and she thought the best place to look was down at Maximo Point in Saint Petersburg, just before the Skyway Bridge.

Everyone went around discussing the last message and looking at the local map I had marked with all the Tocabaga mounds in red. By seven o'clock the whole tribe had decided to meet Sunday afternoon at the Indian Mound Park at Maximo Point.

We all loaded up in our cars and went to Indian Rocks Beach to watch the sun go down. Then it was a mad rush to get Robin home by nine. We had had time to talk and make plans to go shopping on Friday night for more new school clothes for me.

I told her that on Thursday evening I was to meet Ed at seven o'clock to learn how to close the station evenings at eight o'clock during the week when I would be working.

After dropping Robin off at her house, the drive home always seemed longer than expected.

This time, as I was driving home, I passed Joey and Martha on the side of the road. I pulled over, made a U-turn, and parked behind them. I started to get out when Joey walked over to tell me his Triumph Spitfire just stopped and he needed to get Martha home before her curfew.

Martha hopped in my car and I told Joey that when we got to Martha's house, she should call our mothers to let them know we were going to try and fix the car or tow it to Ed's garage.

Martha directed me to her house. The front light was on when we pulled into the driveway.

Her mom was waiting at the door and Martha tried to explain that Joey's car had stopped running and he was stranded on the side of the road.

She introduced me as Joey's friend and said she needed to call Joey's mom and my mom to let them know we would be fixing or towing the car to Ed's American Garage.

Now calmed by the news, Martha's mom was no longer mad and said she would call our moms.

I said that I needed to get back to Joey and see what we could do with his car. Martha's dad came out and brought me a tow rope and said to have Joey call when he and I got home, no matter how late.

Driving back to Joey, I realized that it would be a good thing to work at Ed's Garage and learn as much as I could about fixing cars. Seemed like good life skills.

I pulled up behind the Spitfire. Joey had the whole hood up and was on his knees tinkering with the two carburetors.

He explained that he thought that the adjustment needle on the carburetor had backed out and the engine was getting too much gas.

He turned both needle adjusters all the way in and then backed them out one and half turns each and asked me to turn the key, making sure the car was in neutral.

Low and behold the car started right up. It ran rough and Joey turned out the needle adjusters another half turn, and it began running smoothly. He put down the hood and asked, "Can you follow me home?"

"Let's go," I answered.

Joey drove as fast as he could and we made it to his house with no problems. He said he would get new springs that went on the needle valve the next day and see me on Sunday.

I got home late and my dad was waiting up. He said that Martha's mom had called so all was good. We talked about the dual carburetors and the needle valves. Dad went on to bed. I took a shower and crashed.

Waking up early on Thursday I felt ready to start the day. Dress, breakfast, and out the door early to pick up Robin and on to school.

My lawn mowing jobs were waiting for me after school. The mowing went fine until the belt that drove the back wheels started to fray and then snapped off.

It took an hour driving to and from the Blue Boy mower shop to get a new belt.

The mower was made right in town, so there was no problem getting the new belt. It was a quick change to take off the old one and replace it.

I finished and had to rush to get a shower in before heading to Ed's by 7:00 to learn the closing procedures for the garage.

I parked my car at the side entrance to the garage and met Mr. Ed waiting for me out front. He first handed me the key to the front door of the garage and made sure I placed it on my key ring.

We went to the bathrooms where I learned how to clean and restock them, and make sure they were both locked before leaving.

I also learned how to close the three pull-down bay doors, the back door, and how they were all locked. Finally, Mr. Ed showed me how to count the money in the till, place it in a bank bag and put the bag in the vault in the back room, close the door of the vault and spin the dial, then lock that door on the way out.

My last thing before leaving, was to shut down the station at the electric panel, walk out the front door, and lock it.

At eight o'clock we were standing on the outside of the door and Mr. Ed was saying goodnight. He assured me that he would be there next Monday on my first night closing.

I drove home in a daze. There was so much to learn, and it sunk in what a great responsibility it was to lock-up the station. Then it was home to have a late dinner of frozen fish sticks and French fries from the oven.

Mom and the sisters cooked while I showered. Eating and talking on the phone to Robin rounded out my day.

Friday brought me another full day of school and chores at home. I was looking forward to seeing Robin for dinner but not so much for the shopping for new clothes for school.

I felt all I needed was a couple more pairs of jeans, another dress shirt, some undershirts, boot socks and skivvies, and maybe a new pair of boots.

I picked Robin up at 6:30 and we drove to the Friday night hang out for dinner, Steak'n Shake. We enjoyed our time eating burgers, fries, and milkshakes in the car.

I thought we would go the Western Wear store to get everything I needed. Robin said it would be better and more cost-effective to go to more than one store.

So, off we went and bought a new dress shirt at one store, socks, undershirts, and skivvies at another. Finally ending up at the Western store for the jeans. The new boots I wanted would have to wait until after I had several more pay days at the garage. The store closed at 9:00 and we still had two hours left to go to the beach, walk the sand dunes, and star gaze.

We lost track of time and ended up having to hurry to get Robin home by eleven o'clock. We drove into the driveway right at five 'til eleven.

At exactly 11:00 the front porch light snapped on and it was a quick kiss goodnight, and she was out of the car and inside the front door waving and saying she would see me on Sunday.

I spent all day Saturday with the uncles. There was so much to learn at the shop and I had a bazillion questions about the work at the garage. Uncle Lew pulled his old Willys WWII Military Jeep into the garage and showed me a list of parts on an engine.

We then changed the oil and oil filter, the gas filter, air filter, rotated the tires, followed by a tune up with new plugs, condenser, and points. Good practice for me.

Sunday. Up, dressed, breakfast, and off to pick up Robin for Sunday school and church. I arrived knowing that I would be taking her little sister with us. Robins' mom and dad were going out to a picnic with friends at Fort DeSoto Park. I arrived at Robin's house to hear loud voices through the front door.

As I raised my had to ring the doorbell the door burst open and out came an angry little sister and a fuming Robin. I jumped to open the back door of the car for little sister and the passenger side front door for Robin. The drive to church was quiet. When we pulled in Robin turned in her seat and spoke. "Little sister, be ready to leave right after Sunday School! Got it?"

Little sister removed herself from the car without saying a word and Robin sat quietly. After some tense few moments she opened the door and got out and I followed her to class. After class we went to the car and waited.

One of the moms who knew Robin came out and said she was supposed to follow us back to her house and little sister would be spending the afternoon with her family.

Little sister got in the car and we drove quietly back to their house. They both got out of the car and I sat and waited, in the hot car.

The other mother pulled in right after us and sat in her car with the air-conditioning and engine running.

Out came little sister and got into the other mother's car. The mother waited there until Robin came out and got in my car. She then backed out of the driveway.

On the ride to the Big Boy's Café for lunch, Robin calmed down and told me what was going on. She told me how little sister had wanted to go with us and not to Mrs. Turner's house like a baby.

We enjoyed a nice quiet lunch at Big Boy's. The ride to meet the tribe at Indian Mound Park at Maximo was a short one.

Arriving at the Indian Mound Park located in Maximo, we were surprised to see a blue Mustang convertible with Martha and Joey sitting inside it.

I hollered out the window at Joey, "Did somebody win the lottery or did your mom really let you drive her car?"

Joey just smiled and said, "I hope you will soon be working at Ed's Garage and learn how to rebuild the carburetors on the Spitfire."

Tommy and Janie rolled up in his old Ford Falcon pickup and right behind them Billy and Jasmine. With the whole Tribe gathered, it was time to search for the next clue.

Jasmine took out a copy of the last clue and read it to us all standing at the bottom of the pathway that led to the top of the shell mound.

"You have pulled the sword from its home. The clue did not fall far from home. Head south you will find another mound to explore and there you will find what you are looking for!"

Each pair separated for the search, for what, we had no idea. Tommy and Janie started out to circle the mound to see how much of it had been disturbed. Martha and Joey said they were going to climb to the top of the mound and see what was on top. Jasmine and Billy said they were going to look for another mound that was suggested nearby from what she had read. Robin and I started looking at the trees and doing our best to judge their ages.

After an hour or so everyone was hot and sweaty. No one had found a thing.

That's when an old guy wearing sunglasses and a funny looking floppy hat came wandering through muttering about the oldest trees that had come down in the last hurricane and were piled at the back of the park.

We all spoke at once. We had found a clue in the rubble at Wall Springs, so maybe, just maybe, we would find something hidden in the old tree logs.

Away we went with Tommy going back to his truck to get an axe he always carried there. He came around to where the rest of us were looking and started tapping on the logs looking for and listening for a hollow sound. He recalled that in the past people placed things in the hollowed-out spaces in trees.

Tap, tap, tap, and a yell was heard from Tommy. "I think I've got something, come here and help me roll this log over."

With everyone's help we were able to roll the log over. What we discovered was not only a hollowed-out space but a small metal bank with a combination lock on the front.

Billy was the strongest person there and he did his best to get the dial of the lock to move. No such luck. It had become solidly rusted shut.

Janie yelled out, "We're late! We're late! We have to get a move on if we are going to get home on time. Did you all forget it's Sunday dinner and tomorrow starts another school week?"

With great disappointment, the bank was handed over to me to take to the garage and see if I could get it open on Monday.

The drive to Robin's was faster than I would have liked but we made it on time.

I had just enough time to get home for dinner. I carefully wrapped the bank in some rags I had and placed it in the trunk of my car.

WEEK 12

THE START OF another week. Get up, get dressed, a quick cup of coffee with toast, then off to pick up Robin.

On the way to her house, every time I turned a corner the sound of that old bank clunking around in the trunk echoed loud and clear. It was hard to believe something that small would make that much noise.

When I got to Robin's house, I jumped out of the car and popped open the trunk. I reached in to retrieve the bank, threw it into the front seat, and headed to the front door. I barely got my hand up to knock when the door opened. Robin said goodbye to her mom, and we walked quickly to the car. On school days she always wore shoes and her hair was dry.

I opened her door, and ran around to the driver's side. When I had gotten in and started the car, Robin

held up the old rust-encrusted bank with its door
hanging wide open.

It seemed that the rolling around in the trunk had
sprung the lock and Robin was looking at its contents.
I backed out of the driveway and headed to school.

I kept driving so, we wouldn't be late while Robin
continued inspecting the inside of the bank. No money,
only a square piece of oiled leather that when carefully
opened revealed what we both hoped was the very
last clue.

We arrived at school running a little behind because
of a long train on the tracks we had to cross to get into
the school parking lot.

Robin placed the bank and it's inside treasure into
the glovebox and I locked it inside. Safe and sound!

It was another long day at school. Hot, muggy, and
boring. After school was over, we met at the car for
the drive back to Robin's house. It was full of questions
of what to do with the bank and how to handle the
leather note.

We decided she would take the bank and it's note
inside with her to her house. After her homework was
done, she would do her best to decipher whatever had
been written on the leather.

I left Robin off at her house with the bank tucked
inside her big purse and drove home to change into my
new work clothes and get to work.

I arrived just five minutes early dressed in my new uniform. Ed had sent the mechanic on home. He said he would stay with me my first night to just shadow and watch.

He made big pot of fresh coffee and sat behind his desk in the office smoking a Marlboro and reading the newspaper.

While listening for the bell to ring telling me that a car had pulled up and needed gas, I started cleaning the women's and men's bathrooms. They weren't too bad. A quick mop and refill the paper products and it was out to clean up the three garage work bays that were used that day. Sweeping with the big broom didn't take long. Then, restock the cold drink machine, remove the money from the collection box, count it, log it in on the tally sheet, roll what coins needed to be rolled and place it all in the money sack to be stored in the vault.

Not too many cars stopped by for gas, so it wasn't too hard to get everything done before eight o'clock and closing time.

By the stroke of eight, I had the register counted, tally sheet made, and was walking everything to the vault in the back room.

Ed met me at the door and said I had done a good job and I would be by myself evenings the rest of the week.

I pulled down the bay doors, locked them and closed the office door and turned the key. Ed got in his car and I in mine.

On the drive home, all I could think about was what could possibly be on the piece of leather that had been stuffed inside the bank. There would be no privacy to phone Robin so I would have to wait until morning to get her ideas.

Arriving home, all I wanted was a shower and some dinner. Fish sticks and French fries would soon be my staple meal after work during the week. After dinner I would head to my room to do homework and crash.

The next day started out on a wrong note. I got up to find my dad outside changing my right rear tire. It had gone flat overnight. Luckily the spare in the trunk was in good shape and we were able to get it put on and me on my way pretty quickly. We placed the flat tire in the trunk. I would learn later that day at work how to fix it myself. The joys of owning my own car, according to dad.

I arrived at Robin's right on time. She was waiting at the door with a bigger handbag than I had ever seen her carry before. I opened her car door, and she got in. I walked around, got in, and started the car.

Backing out all I wanted to know was, had she been successful in deciphering whatever was on the leather?

She told me about having to press it out flat and when she had used a hot iron to dry it out some the letters popped out bold as could be. She read these words:

"Clearwater Bay is where we would stay. To fill our casks and make them last. The spring at the bottom of the hill is where we would drink our fill. The plunder that has made you wonder is under the red stone square."

When she had finished, she almost screamed, "Do you know what that means?"

"I don't think so."

"The treasure is there at the bottom of the bluff in Clearwater!"

When I pulled into the parking lot, I turned to her and said, "Lock everything in the glove box and tell no one, not even the rest of the Tribe. We have to keep this to ourselves until Sunday. Can you tell the girls that there won't be any meeting on Wednesday because I have to work until 8:00 every night? Tell them that it would be great to see everyone on Sunday. Maybe we could all meet by the statue at the bottom of the hill next to Pete's Diner."

She looked at me and matter-of-factly replied, "I can do that." What she didn't know was if she could keep the secret until Sunday after church.

The rest of the day poked along until it was time to meet Robin and drive her home.

When I got to my car, she wasn't the only one there waiting. The whole tribe was there standing and sitting on my car.

"What's this I hear about you, you little industrialist!" shouted Joey. "Going and getting a job so we can't meet on Wednesday nights and or even on Friday nights?"

I replied, "We can all meet on Friday nights. I get off work at eight and if one of you could pick Robin up at her house, I could meet you at McDugles as fast as I can get there."

Billy said, "No problem! Jasmine and I will pick Robin up on Friday night. Her house is on the way."

Jasmine looked at Robin and smiled saying, "Yeah, we can do that. What a great idea!"

Now that that was settled, Tommy spoke up and asked, "Were you able to get the old, rusted bank opened?"

Robin looked at me, and I at her.

Robin spoke first saying "We need to get going so D.W. isn't late for work. I promise I will share the complete story on Friday night.

Martha said, "I am okay with that, and I am looking forward to a shared date night with everyone and hearing about the rusty old bank."

Martha pulled Joey from my front fender, and they headed to his car. Everyone else followed suit and Robin and I took off to her house.

Robin said, "Boy that was close. I'm not any good at keeping secrets, but I understand why it is so important at this time."

The rest of the drive to Robin's was made up with her unlocking the glovebox and stashing the bank in her big purse she had been carrying all day. I dropped her off and made it to work right at the stroke of 4:00.

Ed was walking out as I was walking in saying it was his bowling night and if I needed anything he would be at the Lanes downtown and gave me the number.

I told him I needed to plug my tire that had gone flat, and he said, "Read the directions on the glue can and you won't have any problems. Everything you need is laid out next to the tire changer. Put everything back where you found it."

Ed left and I unloaded my tire and set it inside bay two where the tire machine was located. Then I started the night's work. I was able to get everything done by seven o'clock and still pump gas for customers in between.

I read the directions on the glue can and they made no sense at all to me. It made no sense to me to push a rasp into the hole making it bigger. Then using another what looked like a screwdriver with a slot cut into it, shove a piece of rubber with glue on it into the hole. I didn't want to call Ed or my dad, so I called Robin's dad.

I was in luck; he was home and answered the phone. I explained my situation and he said stay right there. He would be over in about ten minutes.

He showed up just like he said he would and walked me through the procedure. It was so easy that I couldn't believe it.

He then turned to me saying he had to get going because he had told everyone at the house he was going out for a carton of Chesterfield's.

I said thanks about a million times as he got in his car and he said, "Remember I was never here."

"Got it!" I shook my head and started the walk through to close the garage up for the night.

I was tired when I got home. Sure, hope I get used to these long days. Shower, dinner, homework, crash.

The rest of the week was the same old, same old with Robin and I doing our best to keep quiet about our discoveries until Friday evening. We both found ourselves clamping our lips or biting our tongues more than once.

Friday night I closed the garage right at the stroke of eight o'clock and went into the back storage area where there was a huge sink and did my best to get cleaned up. I stripped down and changed into a pair of blue jeans and a clean T-shirt. It only took a few minutes. Checking to make sure everything was locked tight I was on my way to McDugles by five after eight.

When I pulled into McDugles I could see that everyone was there already, and that Billy and Jasmine had picked up Robin. Everyone was having what they called a "snack". I ordered my dinner. As I slid into the booth next to Robin, the first thing I heard was, "Okay you two spill the beans!"

I looked at Robin and she told the whole story about the old bank rolling around in my trunk and knocking the rust off, her picking it up off the front seat spinning the tumbler and the gate opening.

She told them about drying the leather sheet and pressing it with an iron and the boldness of the letters when the parchment was dry.

The tribe was at their wits end and only wanted to know what the heck the words said. Robin took a piece of typing paper that was folded up in her tiny purse and read:

"Clearwater Bay is where we would stay. To fill our casks and make them last. The spring at the bottom of the hill is where we would drink our fill. The plunder that has made you wonder is under the red stone square."

Janie shouted, "That's why you wanted us all to meet on Sunday afternoon at Pete's Diner!"

"Not so loud!" exclaimed Robin.

Everyone huddled up close so we could make plans to meet on Sunday and then we all filed out and went on our own Friday night dates.

The first words out of Robin's mouth as we got into my car were, "You still smell like grease and oil! You are going to have to scrub better next time before we go out. I can't go home smelling like a garage!"

"I scrubbed as good as I could in the backroom sink to get here quicker. I think what you are smelling are my work clothes and boots in the back seat."

"Would you, *please*, put them in the trunk?" she asked with a smile.

I had backed out of my space at McDugles, so I put the car back into drive and pulled it back into the parking space and got out.

Martha yelled out the window, "Is something wrong?"

I walked over and leaned in her window and said, "Everything is all right. I just need to put my smelly work clothes and boots in the trunk so they don't stink up the car."

With that, Joey let out a laugh and the clutch on the Spitfire and they were gone in a flash. I opened the trunk and retrieved the smelly offenders from the back seat. All while Robin spritzed some of her perfume to make the whole car smell girly. *I might need to get an air freshener to hang on the rear-view mirror.*

Back in the car I asked, "Where to?"

As we drove out of the parking lot, I saw a pick-up truck parked in the back lot. It looked familiar, like I should know who drives it. But I was with Robin and wanted to get going and didn't put any more thought into it.

"Just drive."

I drove down the old beach road that would take us towards her house.

When we were near the city pier, she asked, "Why don't you park, and we can walk and talk?"

The conversation was all about what she was expecting on her Saturday. She said that she had been volunteered to watch the young kids next door while the parents went out for the day. They could be a handful.

When she was done, she turned to me and asked, "Why are you so quiet?"

"It's only been two weeks and I am already burnt out from learning everything I need to know for the gas station and am afraid that I am not doing a good job at anything."

We walked quietly listening to the waves that rolled into the pier. Before either of us realized it, time had passed, and we would have to make a sprint to her house to get her home on time.

The drive to her house was mostly silent . As I pulled into her driveway the porch light snapped on, which meant there would be no time for conversation. Before I could set the parking brake, she kissed my cheek and was out the car door and inside the house. Her dad waved out the open door as I backed out and headed home.

Saturday was long one. The work hours on Saturday were 7:30 to 4:00 with a half-hour for lunch. When the morning was inching toward noon, Ed asked if I wanted to stay a little longer in the afternoon to help scrub the garage floors.

I replied, "Sure, why not?"

A full day of running to put gas in cars, clean windshields, check tires for air-pressure, and figuring out where all the different car manufacturers had hidden the gas tank covers was exhausting. One car's gas door was behind the rear license plate. While another was hidden under the left rear tail fin. If I was lucky, it would have a simple door on the side of the car in clear sight.

At 4:00 we started to pull everything out of the garage bays. Ed showed me how to mix the degreaser we would be using in buckets of water to scrub the floors.

Then it was scrub with an eighteen-inch wide, stiff bristle brush that was attached to a six-foot handle.

The degreaser did an okay job of getting the grease and oil up with help of the scrub brush. It was hard, wet work. I would need to add a pair of rubber boots to my wish list.

Next, I used the high velocity water hose to rinse out the bays.

I learned how to use the big squeegee to push the excess water out and down the street toward a storm drain.

Just when I thought we were all done Ed said, "Lets push everything back into place and call it a day."

When everything was finally back in place, Ed said, "I really appreciate you staying late to help me. Enjoy your Sunday off. You are doing a great job."

I looked at my watch; 7:00. Talk about a long day at work. I had been on the clock for eleven-hours! *No wonder I was totally exhausted.* Good thing I hadn't planned on seeing Robin. All I wanted was to go home, shower, eat, and conk out!

Sunday morning the sun was up and shining through the window in my room calling me to get moving. I dressed quickly in my Sunday clothes, ate a fast breakfast of peanut butter toast, and headed out the door.

When I pulled into Robin's driveway to pick her up for church I was met by her dad in the driveway.

He came over to the car and said Robin wasn't feeling well and would see me Monday morning if she was better.

"I'll have her call you later, okay?"

All I could think of to say was, "Sure. Tell her I hope she feels better."

I changed my mind about going to church and drove home. I was in my room changing when dad walked in and asked what was going on and why was I home.

As I hung up my dress clothes, I told him what Robin's dad had said and that's when I decided to just drove back home.

Dad said, "Well, since you are home, can you help me change out a coil spring on the old Chevy?"

I followed him out to the garage where he already had the Chevy up on jack stands so we would be able to get underneath it.

Everything was going well, and we were working together, something that we hadn't done much of in the past.

We had to compress the old spring with some home-made screw jacks. That part went smoothly. All we had to do was break loose one rusted nut and remove the bolt.

Looked easy enough. Dad said for me to hold the cold chisel and he would hit it with the short, handled sledge to break it loose.

I tried to reach out with my right hand but couldn't turn my body far enough. I used my left hand to hold the chisel and when it was in place, Whack! Dad had misjudged and hit my hand.

I yelled and reached for the chisel and said, "Hit the chisel this time."

He did and we finished the job. By the time we were done, my four fingers on my left hand were swelling and my whole arm, wrist, and hand ached.

Dad said as he looked at my hand, "I am pretty sure all four fingers are broken. Why didn't you say something?"

"It was fun working together and I didn't want to be a cry baby. I do have a problem though. I need to meet the tribe at two o'clock up in Clearwater."

Without hesitating even a moment he said, "Get in the car. We're going to see Doc Benner." Dad drove to Doc's house a couple of miles away.

When Doc opened the front door to say something to dad, he saw my swollen hand and ushered us to the side of the house where his office was.

Putting all four fingers back in place wasn't a fun experience for me. Every time he pulled a finger to straighten it out it hurt like the devil.

Doc used popsicle sticks on the sides of my fingers to keep them straight. Each finger was taped and then all four were taped together to hold them all straight.

Doc checked them and Doc said I would need to come by on Monday so he could check the swelling and probably redo the tape on the fingers.

Dad thanked Doc who responded that he guessed that his next tune up would be on me.

I told him, "If I can learn how before you need it, I will gladly do it."

Dad said, "Get in the car. We will have to go right now if we are to meet your friends."

We thanked the doctor for taking care of my hand on a Sunday and were out the door and on our way to Pete's Diner to meet the tribe.

As we drove in, Janie saw that I wasn't driving and came over to the car. I introduced dad to everyone and showed them my new stick fingers. All wrapped with sticks and tape.

Everyone was gathered around the car when Tommy started staring at someone across the parking lot by the fountain. He whispered, "Isn't that Buzz, the custodian at school?"

Every one of the tribe, including my dad, looked over toward Buzz. There were several old men with metal detectors moving around the fountain.

Janie spoke first, "I wander if he overheard us talking at school?"

I answered, "I thought I saw his pick-up the other night when we were leaving McDugles!"

Joey spoke up and said, "You know I think I recognize a couple of those guys. They were at the same spots we were at on our Sunday adventures. Do you think they have been following us trying to find the treasure before us?"

"How did they know we that had made plans to search here today across the street at the bottom of the bluff? It sure seems awfully coincidental if you ask me!" Jasmine exclaimed.

Too bad they were looking in the wrong place, I thought. *Or maybe that's a good thing.*

Dad stated , "I need to know exactly what you all are up to, and right now. Tell me everything."

They all looked at me as I told dad about the whole treasure thing. I told him about all the places we had been going every Sunday, the clues we had found, and the search for the treasure.

His answer when I was done was, "We need to throw them off the scent. Let's regroup at our house. Let's go now."

Dad and I got in his car obviously with him driving. The rest of the tribe loaded up in their own cars and left in different directions driving crazy routes back to our house.

When everyone had made it to the house, dad had to do some quick talking to mom about why I didn't go to church, my broken fingers, the visit to the Doc, and why all my friends were here at our house.

Mom wasn't happy with what she heard. With her hands on her hips, she said, "Don't you all know it's Sunday?"

When things died down and everyone had a cold glass of iced tea in hand, dad had a question. "The house you found the box in, do you know who it belonged to?"

Shrugging, my answer was simply, "No idea!"

"Don't you think it would be a good idea to find out the history of that old house to see who owned it and when? Would it be worth it if I went to the City's Hall of Records and looked it up on Monday?" Dad asked.

The whole Tribe responded with a collective, "YES!"

That decided, everyone left to enjoy the rest of the afternoon with their partners and Sunday dinner with their families.

I spent the rest of the afternoon with my hand raised on a pillow with an ice pack on it and wondering if I would still be able to work at Ed's next week. Would I be able to drive? *Good thing it was my left hand and not my right.*

WEEK 13

MONDAY MORNING I arrived at Robin's to find her ready to go to school with a huge smile plastered on her face and just as big a list of questions when she saw my hand. On the drive to school, I explained my taped hand and the excitement about what we found at the site in Clearwater.

I told her about seeing Buzz, the custodian from school, and his cronies there with metal detectors. I told her about my dad going to the City Hall today to look up who had owned the old house and when they had lived there. I told her about the plan to feed Buzz, the custodian, and his guys some false information about what we had found out so far by dropping a written note with a hand drawn map, drawn just for them.

The plan was I would pass the note to her as she was walking into the school and she would let it slip out of her book where she had placed it. Not paying attention that it would happen right in front of Buzz.

We were no sooner parked in the school parking lot than we saw Buzz pushing a broom, watching us as we got out of the car and walking towards the entrance of the school.

Before we got out of the car, I told Robin I would hand her the note and map when we walked in front of Buzz on the way down the hall toward the classrooms.

As we walked in the front entrance, I slipped Robin the note along with a map I had made on Sunday evening. We soon would know for sure if we were being followed or not.

Walking away from me, she pretended to put the map and note in one of her books. She kept walking as the papers floated out of their hiding place in her Science book. Later, she told me it was really hard to walk away and pretend not to notice the papers lying on the ground.

Buzz snatched the note and the map in what seemed like even before they had hit the ground. He looked at it and by the expression on his face he realized it must be the map to the treasure. Looking all around, he stuffed everything inside his shirt and walked away like his pants were on fire.

I had been hiding around the corner watching the whole thing. I didn't catch up with Robin until we were at lunch. It was time to set the next part of the plan in motion.

I had made three other maps for the tribe. The instructions were for them to go to where their maps were marked on Wednesday or whenever they could before Friday evening.

After school, Robin met me at the car to drive her home. As she got in the car, she said she had given the other maps to the girls with instructions to do their best to visit the locations before Friday evening. I had never seen Robin laugh so hard as that afternoon when she said we were playing "I Spy" in real life.

I stopped by the doctor's office on the way home and he re-taped my fingers. The swelling was almost gone, but it would be a few weeks before they were completely healed.

I arrived at work, meeting Ed as he was about to leave. He looked at my hand and said that my dad had called and told him the story of the broken fingers and thought I would still be able to pump gas and do what-ever needed to be done. Ed mentioned with a grin that the restrooms needed a good cleaning and he would see me tomorrow. He left and I got to work.

Pumping gas and getting the rest of the work done with a bum hand wasn't an easy task. By the time it was time to close the garage all four fingers were throbbing.

The rest of the week rolled by with several sightings of Buzz following me around. Some nights I was able to call Robin during the week after work.

She reported that the other girls were calling her with information about visiting their map sites and the sightings of the old cronies at each site. Everyone was enjoying playing undercover spies.

The decision to meet at my house for burgers on the grill after I got off work on Friday was a great idea. Tommy and Janie would pick up Robin on their way and I would hustle home as soon as the station closed.

Friday night I locked the station right at the stroke of eight o'clock and drove home. I walked in though the garage and was met by Robin who exclaimed, "Get scrubbed up and use lots of soap, you stink!"

I showered and put on clean clothes and was greeted with a big hug and the smell of dinner on the grill. As everyone ate burgers and drank sodas, dad told the story of what he had found out at City Hall.

He started with a story of being followed by an old timer who followed him inside the building all the way to the Tax Collectors office.

Dad said he took a number and sat down and waited. The old timer left after ten minutes.

Then he went to the where the titles and deeds were kept and looked up the address of the old house.

The old house where I had worked most of the summer and found the box was built in 1917 by the town's librarian and her sister, Megan, and Martha Blocker.

The house was then sold to the Smith family in 1953 and had sat empty since 1959, after what was described as a strange fire in the kitchen.

Dad said he thought it was a dead end. But when he was back at work his boss asked him why he had gone to City Hall on his lunch break. Dad said he was looking into the background on that old house I had worked on all summer.

Old man Sampson had been sitting out front of the garage smoking his nasty old Camel cigarettes and overheard dad and Mr. Bonds, the owner of the garage, talking.

Mr. Sampson was as old as dirt and had stories about the town where we lived on every subject, including the old house on the bluff.

We all had heard him tell some whoppers and some stories that were basically true.

When were all sitting at the table, dad started telling Mr. Sampson's recollection of the house and the Blocker sisters, "It was a long time ago when there was no city to be found between here and there.

Mr. Sampson had told him the original owners, the Blocker ladies, were both blond and sailed a shore schooner. They docked it there at an old pier down from the bluff. It was deemed strange by the town folks that neither one ever married and would sail that schooner all by themselves.

Dad went on to say, "It's been said that they used gold to build that house there on the bluffs. Real gold in small ingots that had to be weighed by the bank to get their worth. There was many a story that they were descendants of a lady pirate. A blond lady pirate that used the bluffs of Clear Water as her hideaway."

When the tribe heard those two words—pirates and gold—they started to get restless in their seats. This was more exciting than we could have ever imagined.

Dad said for everyone to settle down and he would do his best to tell the rest of the story as it had been told to him.

It goes like this dad continued, "There was a pirate named the Sea Witch. It was told that this pirate was a lady of the sea and would take ships by force in what we now call the Gulf of Mexico. She was said to have long blond hair and could handle a cutlass as well as any man aboard her sloop.

"She was an expert navigator of shallow water along the coast and had a hideaway with fresh water. It was there in the Gulf that the Sea Witch and crew took a Spanish Galleon that was lying at anchor by surprise.

"The Spanish Galleon was headed back to Spain loaded down with gold and other treasures from Mexico.

"After making away with the Incan treasure off the ship, they put that galleon and its crew to the torch, sinking them somewhere in the Gulf. They then sailed in by the bluff to take on fresh water and to celebrate at the Clear Water Spring.

"The story goes on that the location is or was nestled at the bottom of the slight rise of the coast. Most ships couldn't sail in through the shallows. The winding shallow tunnels were filled with mangroves and oyster beds. No one could follow her."

When dad was through telling us the story, we were all ready to get back out to the bluffs and search. Especially now that we had heard the story and it included pirates and gold.

Once Dad got everyone settled down again, he wanted to hear all about the stories of the maps and being followed around by the old cronies.

The stories were funny as each couple told how the old guys would just happen to show up with their metal detectors to poke around where they had walked and made x's in the dirt. Then they would get in their car and drive around the block and watch the old guys wander back and forth finding nothing

Everyone was laughing so hard it was difficult to calm down and discuss where we would meet on Sunday afternoon.

It was decided that we would meet at Pete's Diner again with everyone parking someplace different and walking to the restaurant. Robin and I would meet them there with my own metal detector.

It was ten o'clock and everyone wanted to go off and finish their Friday date night. Robin and I stayed to clean up and have some personal time.

When the dishes were done, and everything cleaned up, we walked over to Uncle Warren's so I could show her what I was making in the wood shop. The pig cutting board had turned out really well and she thought it would be a good present for someone.

Glancing at my watch I noticed that it was time to drive her home. Dad met us in the driveway. He reminded me that we had better get going.

We were at her house early and the front light didn't snap on at 11:30. We guessed that her mom wasn't home.

I knew I had to get home and get to bed. It would be an early morning and a long day at work. We said our good nights with a promise to see each other on Sunday.

On the drive home, I kept seeing a bright red Ford F150 in the rear-view mirror. It would come up and then drop back. I wouldn't see it for a little way and then it would appear in my rearview mirror again. It followed me all the way to the dirt and shell road I lived on.

Once at home I headed straight to bed. Saturday would come quick, and it would be a long one.

Saturday went as well as expected. Pumping gas, checking tires, checking oil, and cleaning windshields all with my bum hand. It didn't hurt too much but it *was* a long day.

Ed had seen my metal detector in my car and asked what was up with that. I told him that it wasn't working right and hoped that all it needed was some new batteries. He said he had always wanted to use one and maybe he could figure out why it wasn't at its best. Taking it out of the car, Ed sighed and remarked at what a beauty it was. I handed it over to him as I went back to pumping gas and checking tires.

Later in the day I saw that Ed had the battery box open on the metal detector. He said that one of the wires had corroded and needed to be soldered back on.

In no time at all he had soldered the wire and placed some protective tape around the connection.

Then he was all smiles. He was like a little kid, out locating every piece of metal in the lot next door to the station.

As we were closing for the day, I thanked Ed for fixing the metal detector. He said that it had been his pleasure and the most fun he had had in a very long time and maybe he could use it again sometime.

I nodded in agreement, and we got in our cars. I headed home for a shower, dinner, and sleep.

Sunday emerged with a beautiful sunrise to announce it. The drive to Robin's was unfollowed by a red pick-up truck or any other vehicle. It was so peaceful.

I arrived at Robin's house to find her ready to go to church. I got out and went around and opened the passenger door for her to get in. The drive to church was animated. Robin asked if I had seen the news.

"No, what's happening?"

She told me, "Today's paper had a story about two old guys including Buzz had been arrested in Clearwater after they had dug a hole and broken a water line by the statue across from the bluffs.

Two others had been arrested for trespassing and relic hunting on the Tocabaga Mound in Safety Harbor, two more at the mound at Maximo Point."

I thought about that for a minute and had a good laugh.

She went on to say, "Each team had a hand drawn map in their possession."

I had never had such fun at Sunday School or church. I couldn't keep the grin off my face when I thought about those old guys using my maps and getting arrested.

After church we drove back to Robin's house with her little sister in tow. I waited in the car for Robin to change clothes. We were just backing out when her mom and dad pulled in.

I waited when I saw her dad wave to me, saying we needed to talk. I put the car in park and set the brake. He walked over and said that local police Chief Swilly had stopped him in the hall at church and wanted to know about treasure maps.

I did my best to keep the story short and he listened with a huge smile on his face. He asked, "Is that what you all have been doing every Sunday?"

"Yes," I replied simply.

"Wait until I tell her mom. She thought you two were doing something entirely different."

He was laughing so hard when he walked away. Robin just looked at her dad and then me and said, "Drive!"

On the drive to Pete's, I asked Robin what was wrong.

She said in a stern voice, "I don't want to talk about it." She continued with, "Just concentrate on what we we are about to do. Find the treasure."

We pulled in a bit late to find everyone else already at Pete's. Lunch was ordered and we wolfed down our food faster than I could ever remember. Then it was out to the car to get the metal detector.

The bluffs where we were sure the treasure would be found had been reworked over the years. They looked different than in the days of pirates. We gathered at the center of the bluffs and spread out in a line.

We had no sooner started when Chief Swilly pulled up in his police car. He walked up, hands on hips, frown on his face and said these words, "You all know you are on City property. Right?"

"Yes, Sir," we answered in unison.

"I suppose you have a map?" he asked.

"Yes, Sir," I replied.

"Did you draw this map?"

"No, Sir!"

"Did you happen to draw four other maps?"

"Yes, Sir."

"Will you be digging on this site today?"

"Yes, Sir; with your permission."

"Carry on, I will be right here to watch." He said as he found a shady spot to watch from.

With that we started looking once more.

It took about an hour to find where they had capped off the spring. Only a small hole was needed to find it with the metal detector.

Chief Swilly wandered over to check out the hole we had dug and to make sure we filled it back in correctly. The only other thing we could find was a brass plaque on the limestone wall at the bottom of the bluff.

Jasmine was reading it and noticed that it looked loose in the wall.

She called Chief Swilly over who tugged on it slightly and it slid out of its hole smoothly. There attached on the back of the plaque were two keys. Chief Swilly said that they looked like safe deposit box keys. They had some markings that looked like BOL. Chief Swilly said the letters stood for Bank of Largo. It had been closed for years and years.

He thought that unclaimed deposit boxes had been moved to an old safe in the basement of City Hall.

We all looked at each other thinking this was another dead end. As we were wondering what would happen with the keys, a black sedan hotrod with rumbling pipes pulled into the parking lot.

When the driver got out, we were shocked to see that it was Robin's dad. And climbing out from the passenger's side was my dad! Robin and I had never seen that car before. Robin's dad explained it was a project car they had been working on for over two years.

Chief Swilly stepped in to explain what had been found and was turning the keys over to the dads.

One to each to hold until Monday when we would all see if they fit the locks on any of the old deposit boxes in the basement of City Hall. Waiting another day wasn't what the Tribe wanted to hear, but we knew the keys were in safe hands.

The dads made us promise not to reveal their project car to the moms. They said when it was completed, they would show it to everybody.

Chief Swilly and the dads left us standing at the bottom of the bluff wondering how we were all going to miss school on Monday.

It was time for us all to get going for each of our respective family's Sunday dinner. The drive back to Robin's was again full of laughter. Pulling into her driveway we were met by her mom. She was asking a lot of questions, starting with had we seen her husband. I told her I had to get home for dinner when, thankfully, Robin's dad pulled in.

I got back into my car and waved to her dad as I backed out of her driveway. Driving home all I could think about was what would happen in the morning at City Hall.

Dinner was kind of quiet until dad spoke up saying in a slow and meaningful manner that tomorrow morning I would be going with him to work.

"What about his school?" Mom asked.

"He will probably miss the day." Dad replied.

A hush fell over the table, and no one asked any more questions.

Week 14

MONDAY MORNING COULDN'T have come
soon enough. I didn't sleep all night with the anticipation of what was about to happen. I met dad in the
kitchen before the sun had even come up. He said
he needed to go to the garage and finish a brake job
for the mayor before we could meet everyone at nine
o'clock at the Court House.

Off we went to the garage. Dad and I finished the
brake job on the mayor's car with no problems *or acci-
dents*. We both had to get scrubbed up making sure we
got all the grease off our hands. Then change our shirts,
pants, and shoes to be ready for what was to come next.

We met Robin and her dad at City Hall at nine
o'clock sharp. Chief Swilly was there with the mayor.
Neither seemed to be very happy about the situation by
the looks on their faces. The mayor unlocked the front
door and ushered all of us inside. We were met by the

security guard that was on duty, a large rotund man that I was sure couldn't run anyone down if there was a break in.

The mayor told the security guard to stay and watch the lobby until the rest of the staff came in at 10:00.

The mayor led us down a long dark hall that led to a door with no markings on it. He took out a key from his vest pocket and unlocked the door.

As soon as the door opened, he flicked a switch on the wall to turn on the overhead lights and escorted us down the stairs into the underbelly of City Hall. The air smelled dank and musty and there were cobwebs and rat droppings everywhere. We followed in single file with the mayor leading and Chief Swilly taking up the rear.

When we got to where the old safe deposit area was, the mayor spun the dial on the vault several times and pulled the door open.

Inside the vault there was a single old light bulb hanging from a cord on the ceiling. We could see the safe deposit boxes were stacked neatly inside.

The mayor went and found the switch to turn on the light in the subterranean area.

To everyone's surprise the boxes were not stacked in any kind of numerical order. So, one-by-one, we took the boxes out into a work area that had a large oak table and better light so we see could try the keys.

Many of the boxes we discovered looked as if someone had tried to jimmy them open with no luck. We all hoped the boxes we were looking for hadn't been emptied.

Chief Swilly stopped us to call in some people to dust for fingerprints to find out who had been down in the basement. The mayor remarked that only he and the head of maintenance had a key. The Chief went up and found the guard was nowhere to be found. He was gone. The front door was wide open as if the guard had run out quickly, not wanting to be caught.

The rest of us were told to sit tight and not to touch a thing until the detectives arrived.

The mayor ushered us up one floor to a small break-room where we were allowed to have a cup of coffee and a stale donut. Waiting was about as much fun as watching paint dry.

Finally, the detectives said we could go back down into the basement. Now, everything was also covered with dust from the finger printing dust they had used.

The dads looked at the keys to verify the box number we were looking for. Box number seventy-three they agreed. The search was on.

We had spent two hours in the break room waiting and then two more hot, sweaty, and dusty, hours looking for the correct box.

Robin and I had been taking the boxes that had been looked at by the dads, the mayor, and Chief Swilly, and stacking them against the wall in numerical order, as best as we could. We saw Robin's dad lift a box with a shout of joy!

"I've got it! Number Seventy-three!! I've got it!" he exclaimed.

With the speed of light Chief Swilly stopped the celebration. STOP! He screamed. We have to take it upstairs so we can document the opening.

With drooping heads, we headed back upstairs to the mayor's conference room. One of the detectives had an old Polaroid Land Camera, another with a small cassette tape recorder, and still another was assigned to take written notes.

We were finally ready to see what was in the box. Would it be a treasure or nothing but another message.

The dads each stepped forward and inserted their keys and turned them at the same time. We heard the lock click and the box lid was open. My dad turned to me and said, "Go ahead its yours, open it."

With a shaky hand I lifted the lid for all to see what was inside.

There was no note. There were no gold bars, no coins, or jewels. There was only a small black silk bag. I was feeling disappointed when I took out the bag and handed it to Robin. She held it in her right hand and remarked that it wasn't very heavy.

It seemed to have sharp edges inside it and there was more than one thing inside. The Chief laid out a white piece of typing paper on the table and instructed Robin to pour out the contents.

As she pulled the string on the bag, she gasped. Inside the bag was a pile of several diamonds.

More than we could count just by looking. One of the detectives picked one up and scratched the glass top table.

"These are real!" He exclaimed in a shrill voice.

Robin held onto the little black bag. She had noticed a message written on the inside of the bag.

The diamonds were counted and placed into an inventory bag by the lead detective.

The chief said Robin could hold on to the black bag now that it was empty. The chief remarked that the police and the City lawyers would make the decision as to who owned the diamonds. Until then, they would be held as evidence by the police department.

The detectives gave us some of the Polaroid pictures of the safe deposit box, the little black silk bag, and the diamonds laid out on the white typing paper. The pictures were all we had to show for the treasure adventure for now. They said we would get a copy of the notes and the recording as soon as they were transcribed.

We were instructed to go home, not talk to reporters or anyone else about our treasure until the property issue was solved.

"Do you mean we can't tell anybody?" I asked.

"Absolutely not!" answered all of the detectives at once.

The ups and downs of Monday had taken their toll on the dads as well as Robin and me. Robin went home with her dad and me with my dad.

At work, later that day, I did my best to stay busy and not think about what might come next. If we were allowed to keep the diamonds, Robin and I had decided that the diamonds would be divided among the Tribe. If we were not able to keep the diamonds, it would at least be a great story to tell.

As I was locking the doors of the garage a news van pulled into the driveway of the garage. A young lady jumped out of the van, microphone in hand, asking questions a mile a minute. I went as fast as I could and got in my car. Backing out of my parking space, I nearly ran over the reporter who continued asking questions as I drove away. The van followed me to my house where there was another news truck. I pulled into my spot and ran into the house.

Dad had already called Chief Swilly about the reporters. I called Robin and yep, there was a news crew at her house also.

We locked all the doors, closed the drapes, and turned off all the lights like the Chief had suggested. Soon there was a patrol car with flashing lights directing the reporters off our properties.

Tuesday was a nightmare. On the drive to Robin's in the morning, I was followed. They followed me to Robin's house and then on to the High School.

When we arrived in the school parking lot there were people everywhere. They formed a ring around my car. We got out and shoved our way through the school's front doors.

At school, the rumors of the lost treasure ran rampant. The other members in the Tribe were being followed, too. Guess either we were big news, or the news vans had no other stories.

Buzz and his buddies had been interviewed after their arrest at the different locations.

The stories of pirate loot grew by the moment. There had been a lot of news on the local television channels already. We had no idea who had leaked the story to the press.

No sooner had the Tribe walked into school than we were all called to the principal's office and interrogated by the principle.

The only thing we could or would tell him was to call Chief Swilly. We were all escorted out of the building to our cars and told not to come back until we didn't bring reporters to disrupt the school. The principle wasn't happy about the situation.

I drove Robin home and then went home myself. No one was happy with the way things were going.

Going to work, I was met by Mr. Ed in the parking lot with him stating clearly that he would stay with me until an officer could arrive to be at the station.

I noticed the news van and the reporters had set up across the street. When the reporters saw the patrol car pull in and park at the station, they packed up and left pretty quickly.

After work there were no reporters following me home. They were already there. Mom wasn't happy that our names were going to be splattered all over the same newspaper that I used to deliver.

Wednesday morning came with both Robin and
I staying home from school. A smart decision made the
night before by our parents.

Chief Swilly had said there would be a decision by
Wednesday at lunch time about the diamonds and we
were going to hold him to it. This whole treasure hunt
had turned creepy.

Robin called and said she needed to talk to me in
private. Walking across the vacant lot to Uncle Warren's
I couldn't figure out what could she have to say to me
that we had to be so secretive.

Robin picked up on the first ring and said she was
in the hall closet. She went on to tell me about the little
black bag.

When the Chief had let her keep the bag, she folded
it and noticed that there was writing on the inside of
the bag. When she got home, she had turned the bag
inside out and saw not another clue but the exact location of a treasure chest.

*"Under the house as the fire-
place stands. Find the place that
is out of place.*

A steel door under the earth.

There is for all its worth."

As she ran out of breath, she asked if we needed to tell the Chief.

While I had been listening to Robin, dad had walked over.

"You talking to Robin?" He asked.

"Yes, Sir!"

"Tell her that the police can find no relatives, no old robbery cases, and no missing diamonds. The town's lawyers say it is a case of finders-keepers. The diamonds will have to be assessed to find their value and then they will turn them over to you. This case may be complete as soon as next week! The Chief also said that it was okay to talk to the press if you want to."

A jubilant cry came from Robin as we both realized we would be wealthy, whether we sold our share of the diamonds or kept them for later in life.

"We need to tell the rest of the Tribe!" I exclaimed.

"No!" Robin nearly screamed! "We need to go to that old house you worked on all summer and see what is under the fireplace first."

"The place is still under construction so I will need to ask permission from Mr. Collins to be on the property and under the house, don't you think?"

"The less people who know the better," Robin quietly remarked.

"I guess I could stop by and check in on the crew one afternoon. I don't think anyone would think anything about it since I worked there all summer.

"When will you go?

"After work on Saturday. No one will even notice me hanging around to talk to everyone. Then I can crawl under the house through the entrance in the back of the house and check it out."

With that decided we hung up the phone.

My plan was to see if there was a treasure hidden under it, and if there was, buy the house with the money from the diamonds as an investment. After all the work I had done on it, I really liked the place.

The days to Saturday drug on and on. School, work, and doing our best impression of all is well around everyone especially the others in the Tribe.

Saturday was a long, hot day at work. Closing the garage at five o'clock, I didn't go home. It was right to the old work site.

There were a few of the regular guys I had worked with still there and they all were interested in all the stories they had heard about the treasure and diamonds.

I told the story of the hunt as quickly as I could.

When asked why I was there I said that my dad was interested in buying the old house as an investment property and he had sent me to check in on the progress.

The crew left one-by-one and the foreman told me to lock up when I was finished doing the walk through.

I hung inside until I knew the coast was clear and slipped out the back door locking it as I went. The crawl space opening near the door was placed so I could crawl right under the house to where the fireplace foundation was located.

Once there it was no easy thing to uncover the concrete slab. There was dirt that smelled funky but digging down I was able to move the piece of concrete, discovering the steel door.

Using all my strength I pried the steel lid open to see a small, old, wooden sea chest.

Taking it out of the hole was hard. The box was heavy and awkward. Sitting it on the dirt in front of me, I opened the box. There was jewelry, slender gold ingots, pearls, and more diamonds.

Replacing the steel lid and then the concrete slab was much harder than I thought it should be. Covering the spot with the smelly dirt took some time. Then it was covering my crawl trail backwards and retracing the path as I backed out the same way I had crawled in.

Sticking my head out the hole, looking around I saw that the coast was clear.

Darkness was descending and I knew I needed to get out of there with the treasure chest. I had no sooner made it to my car and placed the box on the floorboard when Chief Swilly drove by.

Seeing me pulling out of the old house's driveway, he stopped right next to the driver side door of my car. "What are you up to D.W.?" He asked.

"I just stopped by to see the progress on the house I had worked on all summer. The crew just left and told me I could do a walk though and to lock up when I was done."

"Okay," Chief Swilly smiled. "I guess we can both go home. I hate it when neighbors call in and it's a waste of my time. Good night D.W., see you at the station when I hand over those diamonds. Maybe you should buy this old house, seeing how good it has been to you."

The chief and I both drove off with me wondering what to do next.

For once no one was home when I got there. I took the wooden box and climbed the ladder into the attic over the house.

Carefully, I placed the box in the footlocker I used for summer camp. It was the best place I could think of, and as a bonus, it had a padlock. I went back down the ladder, undressed, shook out the dirt from my shirt and pants, showered, put on clean clothes, and called Robin.

She was beside herself with worry about me and sounded angry. "Where are you? Why haven't you called before now? Are you on your way?"

I answered as fast as I could, hung up the phone, and headed out to my car.

Once again, the drive to Robin's had me wondering what I had done to upset her. She was waiting at the door when I drove up.

Going in to say hi to everyone took some time. We finally escaped and I drove to the county park by the lake.

Once parked and having answered most of the questions being thrown at me, I told of my daring, stealthy, findings. Robin listened and then punched me in the shoulder.

"What was that for?" I whined.

"What are we going to do?" She asked.

I calmly said, "I'm going to buy the house and after some time I will discover the treasure box."

"You mean we must wait even longer?" She wailed!

All I could think of to say was, "Yes, unless you have a better idea."

Moments later the park ranger came by using his flashlight telling us the park was closed and to move on. We went to McDugles, devoured burgers, fries, and a coke and started some future planning until it was time to take her home.

Sunday went smoothly with Sunday School and church. I had lined up two oil changes and one tire rotation at the garage for later in the day. Spending my Sunday afternoon at work felt good since I didn't have to think about anything else.

Robin and her dad came by the garage. It was for his car. I was told to do the tire rotation.

While he was there, he asked what I was going to do with my share of the diamonds. My quick answer was I had no idea, maybe buy some real estate as an investment.

That's when he told me that you had to be an adult to purchase real estate. He told me I could give the money to someone over the age of twenty-one and they could make the purchase.

He went on to say, "Make sure to have a lawyer draw up the papers so ownership would turn over to you when you turn twenty-one.

Another wrinkle in the plans. I would have to speak with someone soon.

Robin stayed after her dad left while I finished the oil changes. We locked all the doors and I drove her home. The conversation made it clear I would have to disclose everything to my dad to avoid problems later.

We pulled into her driveway, and I walked her to the front door. I was still in my work clothes, so I didn't linger long. The drive home was filled with a feeling of dread.

Sunday dinner went okay. Everyone was there. After dinner Uncle Warren asked if he could talk to me out on the porch.

"Sure! What do you need."

"I was over visiting my friend who lives across the street from that house you worked on. I was amazed when he said you were still there after the crew left, and then they saw you talking to Chief Swilly."

"I just stopped to see the crew and to check on the house. Thought I might buy it as an investment when I got the money from all those diamonds we found."

"Huh! So why were you under the house? Checking the foundation?"

"Yea! That's it!"

"Son, I've told you before if you're going to tell a story, tell a good one. Now, tell me the truth," he said giving me a look.

The truth spilled out of me like water from the tap.

With a shrug of his shoulders, he said, "I'll buy the house for you. Now, let me safeguard the box.

I will have my lawyer friend draw up the papers saying the house is yours when you turn twenty-one or at my demise."

I handed him the key to the pad lock.

WEEK 15

THE VERY NEXT day when everyone was gone from our house, Uncle Warren climbed up the ladder into the attic, and retrieved the box from the inside of my footlocker. Climbing down he took time to make sure that no one had come home while he was in the attic. The walk back to his house only took a few minutes. He placed the box in his large gun vault, closed its door and spun the dial. The box was now safe from prying eyes.

Going to pick up Robin for school, not knowing how she would take the news of spilling the beans to Uncle Warren and him going to negotiate the purchase of the house was a long slow ride.

Robin was ready to go when I arrived at her house. We drove to school in silence with about fifteen minutes to spare. I wasn't sure how to start the conversation.

As we sat in silence in the school parking lot, she finally turned to me and asked, "What's wrong?"

I started out slowly telling her everything. As she listened to me tell the news about Uncle Warren and the house, she started to smile. Amazingly, she wasn't upset at all. Instead, she was happy that the plan was moving along.

Uncle Warren was moving quickly seeking out the owner of the old house from Mr. Collins while we were at school. He found out that one of his long-time buddies was the realtor handling the house.

Making the deal went as smooth as silk, according to him. All he had to do was put down good faith money to secure the house. It was a good thing he had a little extra in his bank account.

After school was over for the day, Robin met me at my car in the parking lot. The drive to her house was filled with thoughts about what she would do with her share of the diamonds. I dropped off Robin, went home to change clothes, and headed off to work at Ed's.

I was surprised to see Chief Swilly waiting for me at the garage parking lot.

He was in a good mood with a huge smile on his face as he announced that the city lawyers and the county judge said the diamonds were ours. They had been assessed at one million two hundred thousand dollars and there was a buyer waiting to turn them into cash.

A quick division in my head and I figured each of the Tribe would receive a hundred and fifty thousand dollars.

The house was listed at sixty-six thousand. That meant that even after taxes there would be a little left over.

Hearing the news Ed said, "So, I suppose you won't be working here anymore."

"Wrong!" I replied. "I will still be working, going to school, and being a member of the Gator Tribe. I still have a whole lot to learn."

My evening flew by as the time to close the garage neared. Calling Robin as soon as I got home was the best part of my day. Telling her that everyone in the tribe would be a hundred and fifty thousand dollars richer was a bonus.

When she calmed down, she wanted to know "Do we have to sell the diamonds, or can we just hold on to them?"

"To the best of what I have been told, you can do as you please. The question you need to get answered is how much it will cost to have them cut and made usable since they are still what jewelers call "uncut" and will need to be cut and polished sometime in the future."

After the call to Robin, I had to make the rest of the calls to all the Gator Tribe members. The excitement ran high as each of the tribe realized that they were going to share in the diamonds and the money they would fetch.

Chief Swilly had said we could pick up the diamonds on Friday morning at the police station. The tribe would be invited also as the decision had been made to share the diamonds with its members.

The news in our small town spread like wildfire with the story of the long-lost treasure.

Friday morning at 9:00 the members of the Gator Tribe and our families arrived at the police station. Finding the place mobbed with reporters and news vans from around the county who were doing their best to wrangle one of us and get the story was more than a little unnerving.

Two police officers escorted us into the main hall of the station. Most of us had never been inside the building ever before that morning.

Chief Swilly handed the bag of uncut diamonds to me. Standing next to the Chief was a man in a black suit with an expensive brief case and an armed guard standing next to him. We were introduced to him as the man who wanted to purchase the diamonds. He spoke up saying he would be delighted to write out the checks that very moment.

We took our places. Sitting around a table with the officers standing around the diamonds as they were divided up among the eight Gator Tribe members was really something.

You could have heard a pin drop as the diamond selections were moved in front of each of the tribe.

The girls all decided to keep theirs as stones. The diamond expert placed the stones neatly in little silk bags he had brought with him.

The guys all had other ideas and took the checks. My decision was to sell all my diamonds except one that I thought I might use at a later date in time.

Once the transactions were all completed, we all did our best to escape out the back doors and into our families' cars.

It had been decided that everyone was invited to go to Joey's house for a celebration and barbeque. The celebration and party lasted long into the evening with only the parents staying late. The tribe left for our normal time at McDugles and then got going, each our own way.

All day Saturday at work, out to a movie with Robin Saturday night, Sunday School and church Sunday morning, and a quiet afternoon at a county park.

Life had certainly calmed down.

When we were finally alone, I told Robin that my uncle had bought the house for me, using his own money as a down payment. We still had to get the papers drawn up at the lawyers as soon as possible.

The paperwork would state that the house would be mine if Uncle Warren passed away or when I became twenty-one. She seemed happy, but not completely.

EPILOGUE

IT TOOK ANOTHER week to finalize the sale of the house. Uncle Warren and Uncle Lew would be doing the finish carpentry on the inside of the house. They thought that the baseboards and crown molding needed to match the period of the house.

One of the first things that would need to be done was to install a huge gun safe in what would be my office. We would place the treasure box there. The reveal of its contents would be exposed six months later.

The story would be that when Uncle Warren and I had to do some repairs on the foundation of the chimney, the fire box was discovered.

Inside the firebox we discovered the actual treasure box that had been hidden for all those years.

The realization was the jewels and gold in the box was how the sisters had built the house and lived so comfortably for all those years. Somehow, they had found the Sea Witch's booty.

Robin was the only other person who knew the real story, that I had found the real pirate's treasure. What came next was a complete surprise.

The story broke in the news on a Friday afternoon. Monday morning the state's attorney appeared at my front door. He said that the antiquity act stated that unrecovered pirate treasure when identified would be the property of the state. It was to be to be placed in the maritime museum at the capitol.

We didn't turn over our findings right away but allowed the lawyers to see it through the courts.

After several attempts of the state to seize our findings, they were not successful in proving the box we found under the chimney or the diamonds in the safety deposit box were indeed part of any pirate's treasure. They found they couldn't prove anything. The court's decision was "finders' keepers".

By the end of my school year, life had settled down. The house was bought and paid for. We each had one more year of High School and then I planned to head off to college to get a degree in forestry.

Robin would be off to college to become an interior designer. We would continue to date and be together during our senior year. Dreams were being made and kept. Life was good.

I had no clue what the future would hold. All I knew was it was the start of the next Great Adventure for the Dead End Kid, and I was ready . . .

ABOUT THE AUTHOR

I grew up on a dead-end street, where there weren't many folks. The swamp was a place of mystery and adventure. A place to roam with nobody else butt'n in. A place that a person could live out any and all of their dreams of frontier life, knights of the round table, archaeologists in the deepest darkest Africa, Tarzan, and of course, cowboy life.

With no real friends around, I made my own fun. Climbing the live oak trees that were covered in muscadine grape vines, I found you could walk on top of them from tree to tree, spread a blanket down on top and lay there unnoticed from the ground at night and see every star in the sky.

The swamp held many things. One was my private swimming place. A clear-fed spring that you could see all the way to the bottom and watch the fish that were in it. Now and again a gator might swim by, but they never bothered me.

Over the years, before I had to start working to pay my own way, I built what people call a lean to. It turned out to be a kind of shanty.

I used an old WWII green tarp to cover the roof. *Who says trash pile picking don't pay off?*

I built myself a bed that was on legs lashed together with string from the hay bales they used at the farm next to us.

It is where I first let my imagination roam. It was also the first place I started to write stories. I showed the stories to the librarian in the family and she said they weren't much and maybe I should learn a trade working with my hands. Soon after I put down the pencil and worked every hands-on job there seemed to be. From bagging groceries, pumping gas, all the way to digging holes and climbing poles.

Many years later I got up the courage to write a real book with stories that meant something and might just, maybe, teach a lesson on life for those who read them.

The brand-new adventure starts Right NOW!

D.W.

If you enjoyed this book you won't want to miss the next mysteryin the Dead End Kid Adventures series. To learn more about live events and to discover when I will be in your area, speaking, or at reading events, be sure to visit D.W. (Dick) Powell at:

www.RobRickOutdoors.com

https://fb.me/DickPowell3591

I would also appreciate reading your comments about this book as well as the rest of my books. Please take a moment and leave a review on your favorite online book retailer.

What will be the next adventure for D.W. Patton?

Other Books by
D. W. "Dick" Powell

How Not To Lose Your Bass in Business: Business is Like Fishing was written to help small business owners navigate through the everyday realities of succeeding in business.

Woodscraft Nation was written with the essence of an earlier America and the spirit of adventure with a practical, easy to understand guide to the outdoors. It is a needed resource to rekindle our connection with the Native American culture, surviving the outdoors, and teaching leadership skills that are meaningful and life changing.

DEAD END KID ADVENTURES

Swamp Archeologist While exploring the deep, dark swamp at the end of the road, eleven-year-old D.W. Patton discovers clues to a long-forgotten robbery gone bad. A gravestone with no skeleton and buried treasure set the scene for an exciting adventure.

Kidnapped on the High Plains A young man grows up quickly when kidnapped on a high adventure trip. He must use all of the knowledge and skills learned from the Woodscraft Nation Handbook to survive and escape.

Mystery of the Box Turtle Shell: Finding Samantha D.W. Patton, a young teenage boy, who is led on an adventure after finding a bleached box turtle shell with a message to "Help" and an ID bracelet inside.

D.W. is Available for personal appearances. Topics he can speak to are Storytelling with a Purpose, Storytelling with a Purpose, Keynotes on Leadership, and Personal Coaching.

Contact: DPowell@RobRickOutdoors.com

Watch For Additional books and resources coming soon from RobRick Outdoors

www.RobRickOutdoors.com